SANCTIFIED AND HORNY

Lock Down Publications and Ca$h
Presents

Sanctified and Horny
A Novel by *Xtasy*

Lock Down Publications
Po Box 944
Stockbridge, Ga 30281

Visit our website @
www.lockdownpublications.com

Copyright 2023 by Xtasy
Sanctified and Horny

First Edition May 2023
Printed in the United States of America

This is a work of fiction. Names, characters, places, and incidents either are products of the author's imagination or are used fictitiously. Any similarity to actual events or locales or persons, living or dead, is entirely coincidental.

Lock Down Publications
Like our page on Facebook: Lock Down Publications @
www.facebook.com/lockdownpublications.ldp
Book interior design by: **Shawn Walker**
Edited by: **Sunny Gabriel**

Stay Connected with Us!

Text **LOCKDOWN** to 22828 to stay up-to-date with new releases, sneak peaks, contests and more…
Thank you.

Submission Guideline.

Submit the first three chapters of your completed manuscript to ldpsubmissions@gmail.com, subject line: Your book's title. The manuscript must be in a .doc file and sent as an attachment. Document should be in Times New Roman, double spaced and in size 12 font. Also, provide your synopsis and full contact information. If sending multiple submissions, they must each be in a separate email.

Have a story but no way to send it electronically? You can still submit to LDP/Ca$h Presents. Send in the first three chapters, written or typed, of your completed manuscript to:

LDP: Submissions Dept
Po Box 944
Stockbridge, Ga 30281

DO NOT send original manuscript. Must be a duplicate.

Provide your synopsis and a cover letter containing your full contact information.

Thanks for considering LDP and Ca$h Presents.

Xtasy

Chapter 1
Xzavier

I parked my Porsche truck around the corner from my destination. I turned my truck off and flipped the visor down to double check my appearance in the mirror. My black masquerade mask hid my appearance exactly how I wanted it to do.

A day ago, I was sent an email from someone I didn't know. The email was an invitation to a party. Not just any party, the invitation read that it was a secret, adventurous party. The details were of few, but I was able to read through the lines. I was told to leave my phone at home and to bring as many condoms that I thought I would need for the night. I was told that I could bring a partner. I just didn't have one that I knew would keep everything a secret.

When I first read the email, I ignored it. I already had my own adventurous life. I had sex on a regular basis, with numerous sex partners. They weren't the best sex partners, but they never failed to get the job done. So, what made me go back to the email? I could honestly say that it had to be the freak in me.

When I say freak, I don't mean creepy. I'm abnormal when it comes to sex. It's not the penetration that gets me to cum, or the slippery affects from a woman's tongue. I'm very peculiar when I have sex. In order for me to cum, that is. I have a side of me that I've hid from the entire world. But, before I can tell you about the side of my no one knows about, let me first tell you about the side of me that the world knows. The side of me that I'm not ashamed of.

My name is Xzavier Cornelious King. I am twenty-eight years young, born and raised in Southwest Houston Texas. I have no children, none to my knowledge that is. Don't misunderstand me, I'm not a deadbeat, or a jackass who wouldn't take care of his children. I've always been smart enough to wrap my guy up when it's go time. Safe sex is the best sex, as they say. Honestly, the reason I haven't had any children, is because in my family you have to be married in order to have sex.

That's correct, if you guessed it. I grew up in a church going household. In fact, my father's name is Richard King, who is the proud owner of the second largest church in Houston Texas. My father owns 'The Lords Manna' in Southwest Houston. His church holds over eighty thousand seats and counting. All my life I've been groomed to take over my father's church.

My mother, Rachel King is the first lady of all first ladies. My mother and father have been together since the ninth grade. They said that it was love at first sight, and it's been the same for them every moment they lay eyes on each other. My father preaches marriage before sex because it's what the Bible preaches. My mother, on the other hand, preaches marriage before sex because she says all women should honor their bodies, and that a husband should be the one to bring a woman into womanhood, not just some random man from the streets.

My mother and father both think I'm still a virgin. A twenty-eight-year-old virgin, yeah right! I mean, they do have one good reason that they should believe it, which is because I told them so. My mother and father think that I'm an angel sent from God up above. In their eyes, I'm without a stain or blemish. It's amazing how parents can raise their child and know nothing about them.

My father has been grooming me to take over his pulpit for when he steps down. In truth, if I can be totally honest, I don't want it or anything to do with it. Again, please don't misunderstand me because I do love the Lord, and I appreciate all the blessings he's poured down on my life. But one thing I do know, God punishes the ones that preaches the word and still sin, way harder than a normal sinner. How is it possible? Maybe there are two different levels of hell where the sinning preachers fire is hotter than the rest. And honestly, I don't want to have to be the one to test the flames.

The real reason that I don't want to take over my father's church, is because I'm addicted to sex. When I say addicted, I'm not sugarcoating it. I mean, I need sex to breathe. I go to bed, dream, and wake up thinking about sex. I love everything about sex. The foreplay. The way people's bodies fold in together. The way our bodies sweat when we feel our orgasm coming. Or the way a woman's' mouth forms into an O shape when I'm hitting her spot.

Sex is beautiful in every shape of the word, form and fashion. If me having sex without being married sends me to hell, at least I'll have all of my sexual encounters to masturbate to in hell. I know a lot of women may be thinking, "Why not just get married, and have sex all the time with the wife?" I've thought of that, honestly. I'll be a liar if I said that every woman has some good pussy. And I'll be a liar if I said that I could be content with one woman who does have some good pussy.

Everything in life is meant for seasons. There is a time for everything, and that's coming straight from my fathers' favorite precious book. But a woman's vagina is the same as fruit. I've had a few women tell me, "My pussy taste like strawberries." But women seem to forget that strawberries do go sour. I don't want to marry just because of that. So, what if you do have some good, wet pussy. One day, it's going to go sour, and wells always runs dry, eventually.

So yes, I'm scared of marriage. Not the ring, or the wedding part, but committing my penis to one sole piece of pussy. That shit there scares me worse than living in an eternal pit of flames. The bad and sad thing about everything, I know me not taking over my father's church will most likely break his heart. I've heard that time heals all wounds, but I know a broken heart can never be pieced back together.

Back to the invitation though. When I first saw it on my email, I ignored it. But the freak in me made me go back to it. And now that I'm here at the secret location. My freaky antennas are standing at full attention. I made sure to park around the corner just in case someone was to notice my truck. I stepped out my Porsche truck wearing a black Tom Ford suit, a pair of black Tom Ford loafers, with no boxers on underneath my pants. I walked around the corner to the location. It was in a dark alley; the only building was a tan warehouse. The sign above the door read, Sinners Palace. The alley was deserted, except for me.

I took a deep breath as I stood at the warehouse door. I knocked three times like the invitation instructed, then I waited. A sliding peephole slid open. All I could see was another set of eyes hid behind a blue and gold masquerade mask.

"Password," The doorman said in a deep baritone voice.

I cleared my throat and said, "Reality of Fantasies."

I jumped back as the peephole swiftly slid closed. I stared at the door in silence, then the sound of the locks turned and the heavy door opened. The doorman held the door opened. I briefly looked up at him. He also wore a black suit, just like the invitation had instructed.

As I walked inside, my body began to tingle. I could practically smell the sweet smell of sex in the air. The warehouse was huge. The doorman walked behind me. I hid my eyes from him. I didn't want anyone to notice me. I stepped to the side as the doorman walked past me. I continued to look around. There were no single chairs, only love seats and large king-sized beds. There were over thirty men and women dressed in all black, everyone wore a masquerade mask to hide their true identity.

"Drink?" a naked waitress asked as she held a silver tray with champagne glasses lined up perfectly on it. I looked at her body up and down. She was completely naked. The only things she wore were a pair of high heels, a masquerade mask, and a very beautiful smile. She had a perfect body. I could tell that her titties were fake, but they still looked amazing. Her body was toned, a coke bottle shape I would say. She looked at me with a beaming smile as I stared at her body. I could tell by the way she was smiling that she could tell that this was my first time.

I accepted a glass from her tray and gave her a smile back. I took the glass to the head to gain back my courage. I had never before been nervous in front of a naked woman. But then again, I would always be naked as well.

"I hope you fulfill your fantasy," the waitress said as she sashayed away.

I turned to get a good look at her backside. She looked even more beautiful walking away. I had to shake my head to come back to reality, because in my head, I made her cum on my dick ten times.

I strolled off. I sat my empty glass down on the arm of an all-white couch. As I admired the couch, I noticed there was a man lying on his back, and a woman was riding him in plain sight. I tried not to stare, but the way the woman was moaning grasped my attention. The man gripped the woman's ass as she rode him harder and harder. Watching them made me think of a porn star camera man. I was watching them like I was directing a porn scene.

"Beautiful, isn't it?" a soft voice asked from behind me. I turned around embarrassed, like I had been caught with my hand in the cookie jar.

I cleared my throat. "Uh, yes. It is," I said as I tried to gather myself.

I stared at the woman in front of me. She was about five foot five, estimating. She had long dirty blonde hair with red streaks in patterns. She had dark smooth skin that matched her black dress.

"I can see that you're enjoying yourself," she said as her eyes traveled down to my dick.

I followed her eyes down to my hard-on. I placed my hand over my bulge in embarrassment.

"I-I'm sorry," I apologized.

She laughed and waved me off. "Don't be. If your dick isn't hard, then this isn't the place for you."

The way she said *dick* made mine jump. I had never heard a woman say dick with no hesitation, without being ashamed. Even the women I fucked in the past never said dick. They would always use the word, penis.

"I guess you're right," I said as I moved my hand. She looked at my print, then she licked her lips seductively without looking away.

"Is this your first time?" She asked.

"Yes. Is it yours?" I asked.

She shook her head. "No, I've been here before."

"So, how does everything work?" I asked as I looked around. There were several different groups of people having sex. Some in pairs, others in groups of threes and fours.

"Here at Sinners Palace, everyone's identity is kept safe from the public. There are no phones, cameras, and no boundaries. This is the place of fantasies, and everyone here can be themselves. Some are exhibitionists. They come here to allow others to get off on them by walking around naked. Some people are cucks. Those men come here with their wives and allow them to have sex with other men while they masturbate to their wives getting hammered by dicks bigger than their own. Some women come here to get gang banged by random guys that they'll never ever see again,"

"What about you?" I asked.

"What about me?" She countered.

"What do you come here for? What fantasy are you here to fulfill?"

She smiled, then she looked at me up and down. She held her hand out to me. "Give me your hand, and I'll show you."

I placed my hand in hers as she turned her back to me and led the way. Her dress was tighter than I imagined as I looked at her voluptuous ass. I couldn't make out a panty line, or a thin line, so to my guess, we were both naked underneath our clothes.

We walked past an all-out orgy of ten people on a king-sized bed. I stopped and looked at them in awe as they all sucked and fucked each other. My mystery lady yanked my hand. I snapped out of my trance and looked at her to see the most beautiful smile I've ever seen.

"You're not a virgin, are you?" She asked.

I smiled and said, "If I was, would you take advantage of me?"

She laughed. "No but, I'll let you take advantage of me."

I stepped closer to her and whispered, "Then don't tell no one, but, I'm a virgin."

She blushed as she rubbed my toned arms. She grabbed my hand again and led the way. She led us to a king sized bed in the middle of the room. The bed was roped off. Behind the bed were two metal poles, both had a chain attached to them with a single handcuff on each pole. We entered our private domain. As we did, a small group formed outside our VIP section.

"Virgin boy," she said as she looked at me. "Are you ready?" she asked as she let go of my hand.

I nodded as our crowd of spectators looked on. My mystery woman grabbed my face and kissed me like we didn't just meet five minutes ago. She explored the inside of my mouth better than any dentist ever has before. My hands roamed all over her body. As her tongue explored my body, my hands did the same. Her body felt soft and smooth under my rough hands. As she broke away from our kiss she said," I'm going to take it easy on you, since it's your first time." She winked at me, then said, "But, don't take it easy on me."

My mystery woman stepped backwards, then she turned her back to me. She looked over her shoulder to me and pointed at her zipper. I took ahold of her zipper, taking my time pulling it down. Undressing beautiful women is my major. It does something to the pit of my soul.

I stepped closer, closing the gap between us as I pulled her zipper down to the top of her perfect ass. I knew she could feel my hard-on brush against her ass by the way she moved from side to side, rubbing her soft ass on my print. She took a step forward looking over her shoulder the entire time. I stared in anticipation as she slowly pulled her tight dress down and past her thick, toned thighs. And just like I figured, she was naked underneath.

I could hardly contain myself, I had to see how soft she really was. I placed my hand on her back and she shivered under my touch; I closed the gap between us placing my dick against her bare ass.

"How do you want me?" she asked, just above a whisper.

I placed my lips close to her ear and whispered, "First, on your stomach, legs spread. Then I want to chain you to those poles so that I could devour your insides with my tongue."

She nodded without looking back at me as she seductively walked to the king sized bed. She eased on the bed, knees first, then she laid flat on her stomach. Her legs opened. A light came on above the bed singling us out. I looked over my shoulders to see a larger group than before. There were both men and women staring at me waiting on me to make my move. A few men had their dicks in their hands slowly masturbating. A woman sat on a couch a short distance away. Her legs were spread eagle. She had her hand between her legs, two fingers were slowly moving in and out of her wet pussy as she stared at me, waiting for me to start the show.

I had never had sex in front of anyone, let alone a room full of masturbators. But there was a first time for everything. I reached for my mask, then I stopped myself. Instead, I took off my Torn Ford jacket and tossed it to the side by the bed. Next came my loafers. I slipped out of them quite quickly. Behind me, I could hear the sticky sounds of cum moving up and down on someone's dick.

The sounds of a woman's fingers moving, slipping in and out of her sweet hole. The sexual sounds were my motivation, like my theme song. I unbuckled my Tom Ford belt. I started to throw it to the side, but then an idea came to my mind. I unbuckled my pants and let them fall to the ground. I stepped out of them into a new man. I walked towards the bed with the belt in my hand. My mystery woman spread her legs wider as she felt the bed move underneath her.

"No boundaries, right?" I asked her as I crawled closer to her.

"None," she answered.

I ran my hand all over her soft ass, slowly enjoying the softness of her skin. "Your body is so, soft," I said as I admired her body.

"Thank you. My insides are just as soft, if not softer," she said making me laugh. This was all so different to me. Having sex with a woman who's name I didn't know. A crowd of horny spectators cheering me on with moans of their own. If heaven wasn't like this, I didn't want no parts of it.

I used my belt, teasing her soft skin with the leather. As I teased her skin with the belt, I ran my other hand over her bottom. I could feel the goose bumps under my hand, bumps of anticipation.

"Do you like it rough, or slow and steady?" I asked as I straddled her backside. My hard dick poked at the entrance to her thick thighs.

"Surprise me," she said as I raised the belt above my head. I placed the belt around my mystery woman's head to assist me. I placed the belt securely around her neck. Not too tight to where she couldn't breathe, but tight enough to where she moans and her air circulation would cut off causing for a deeper orgasm.

After I secured the belt, I eased back on my knees to get a closer look at her box. The light above the bed gave me just enough light to see down her tunnel. They say in life you only find true love once. I come here to tell you that that's a lie, because I fall in love with every piece of pussy I've ever encountered.

"Virgin boy, are you going to keep this good pussy waiting all day or are you going to become a man for the whole room to see?" she asked as she got herself comfortable, laying her right cheek on her hand.

I looked over my shoulder at the awaiting crowd. The beating sounds of their hearts made me feel like I was an NBA player at the free throw line, the game is tied up, and if I sink the shot, we'll be world champions for the very first time in history.

I placed my finger at her soft, slippery entrance. I rolled her pearl between my fingers like a basketball player rolls the ball through his hands as he sets up for a shot. My mystery woman moaned under my touch. My dick poked at her entrance, anxious to feel the inside of her paradise. I gripped my dick, angling it up to slide in her hole. As I neared her pussy, I could hear the faint sounds of moans get louder the closer I got. I wasn't the only one in the room getting some action, but I had to be the only one in the room this hard and ready.

I slid my dick inside of my mystery woman. Her ass cheeks tightened as I leaned forward applying pressure to her soft spots. My dick hit the bottom of her pussy in one swift thrust. I felt bitter-sweet as I froze inside of her pussy. I was in a warehouse called Sinners Palace, but I was using my dick God blessed me with to do the devil's work. I never thought it would feel this good being a sinner.

"Fuck me!" My mystery woman moaned, bringing me back to reality. And fuck her I did.

The inside of her pussy felt different. I've had more pussy than I could count, but without a doubt, my mystery woman took the cake. The way that I could feel ripples running down the sides of her walls, that shit had me shivering in the pussy. In a sense, she had me feeling like I was a virgin all over again. Her pussy felt so good, I was already ready to cum.

I took ahold of my belt. The swift motion made her neck jerk backwards. Her head raised up. I had her bent and twisted like a pretzel. I held the belt strap like I was holding on to the reigns of a horse. In a sense I was, because the lady underneath me was nothing less than a stallion. Megan didn't have a damn thing on her.

I used my left hand to spread her ass cheeks so that I could go as deep as I could. The inside of her hole was so pink and wet. The pinkest I've ever seen in my whole life. Her dark, smooth skin brought out her pinkness to another level.

"Virgin boy, go deeper," she moaned. I didn't know where she wanted me to go. I honestly thought I was as deep as I could go. I was smacking the bottom of her pussy with my balls with every stroke.

I used my knees to spread her legs until the point I thought they were going to break. As her legs spread, her ass seemed to raise up. Her pussy began to spread, giving my dick more room to work.

That was why I was head over hills for women. They were special. I mean God did his best shit when he created them. It was something about the way their bodies mold for a man's pleasure. It was honestly a work of art. It was beautiful, beyond exotic. My mystery woman knew exactly how to work her pussy, like hers came with a how-to manual.

Our bodies collided back and forth like a set of bumper cars. Her sweet-smelling juices dripped from her hole to the bed sheets. My dick was coated, creamed with a mixture of our cum. My mystery woman raised up and gripped the sheets. I noticed her nails for the very first time. They were painted all black, with a small red heart on both pinky nails. For some odd reason, I found that extremely sexy.

My mystery woman eased up on her hands and knees. I could tell that my dick felt good to her because she wasn't able to get a single word out. The only thing that came from her mouth were slow passionate moans. Her head would fall forward, but I would yank it back up by pulling on the belt strap. I felt myself about to cum. My eyes closed tight. The pressure was building to the point of no return. Then, I remembered I didn't have on a condom.

My eyes shot open as I felt hot cum shoot from my hard dick. I pulled out as fast as I could. My semen shot in the air like missiles as my semen landed on her ass cheeks. I looked at her gaped hole, it was wide open. It seemed to be breathing, panting, as if it was trying to catch its breath. I licked my lips as I watched my hot cum seep from her glistening hole.

My mystery woman stood up and looked into my eyes. She wore the prettiest smile on her face. God, how I wanted to take off her masquerade mask to see how beautiful she really was. Then, I thought that maybe she was hiding her beauty for a reason, like me. Maybe she had people that would judge her for the nasty, but sincere things she loved to do with her body.

My mystery woman walked to the two posts behind the bed. She cuffed her right wrist, then she looked to me for assistance. My dick was semi-hard. Cum dripped from the head like a dog drool from the corner of its mouth. I walked up to her. She had a look in her eyes. A look of want. A look of desire. A look of fulfillment. And I was the only one that could fulfill her want. I was the only one that could fulfill her desire. I was the one she chose to make her fantasy a reality.

I stepped up to my mystery woman like I was stepping up to the plate to bat. She looked deep into my eyes, like she was trying to see the man behind the mask. Like she was trying to reveal my true identity. I stood face to face with her. With her free hand, she grabbed my limp dick and stroked it slowly. Her soft, small hand felt electric. Waves of pleasure shot through my dick, reviving it back to life. I brushed my lips against hers. A soft peck on the lips, then another.

I looked at her as her eyes slowly closed. I began to wonder, was this her fantasy. To meet a guy, and have him make her feel empowered. But at the same time, feel helpless. I bit her bottom lip as my fingers brushed against her swollen clit. Her head fell back in bliss as I grabbed her left hand.

I cuffed her to the tall post as her eyes began to open. No longer was there a look of empowerment. No, that look had gone, and it was replaced with a look of desire.

I kissed her once more as I then circled her. I admired every inch of her body as I circled her. As I stood behind her, I unbuckled the belt around her neck. I removed the belt and rubbed the spot where the belt had been, then I kissed her neck.

I stood on the side of her. She turned her head to look at me. "What are you about to do to me?" she asked.

"I'm about to punish you for your sins," I replied. I pulled my hand back with the belt in hand. I came forward full force, spanking her with the belt. My mystery woman yelped out loud as the belt made contact with her bare ass.

Onlookers stood up from their seats. Some walked to get a closer look as others walked past the roped area. Two men and three women climbed on the king-sized bed we had vacated. They fondled each other as they watched us. They looked at me like I was God. Like I had come to set them free. Another woman kneeled in front of my mystery woman. She kneeled right in front of her wet pussy. My mystery woman opened her legs wider. The woman kneeling opened her mouth wide and kept it open. A different woman strutted over to me. She was Caucasian, with long dirty blonde hair. She was completely naked, except for her three-inch heels, and the blonde landing strip of hair on her pussy.

The blonde woman kneeled in front of me. She grabbed my dick and placed it in her warm, wet mouth. She used her supreme head game to bring me to my tiptoes. I looked around the room. I felt great. This was my church. I was the preacher. And my spectators were my congregation. I looked at my mystery woman, my potential first lady. She stood chained to the poles, anxious, waiting on me to judge her for her sins.

I brought the belt back and looked around. Everyone seemed to be waiting one me. I let my arm swing. My mystery woman cried out. I swung again, this time a little harder. She yelped out for the entire room to hear. Her head fell forward as she panted. I pulled back, belt in hand. I looked around, then I looked down at the woman that had my hard dick in her mouth. She looked up at me with tears of joy in her eyes.

I let my arm fly. The force that came behind the blow took all the energy out of my body. As the blow landed, both me and the mystery woman cried out. My second orgasm of the night shot straight down the pretty blonde woman's throat. At the same time, my mystery woman squirted. Her watery cum squirted into the awaiting kneeling woman's mouth. My mystery woman's orgasm caused her to shake as she was attached to the chains. She looked possessed.

My eyes closed as my knees began to feel weak under me. A loud applause erupted bringing me back to reality. I opened my eyes. I was no longer in Sinners Palace, but in my father's church.

Xtasy

Chapter 2

"I said, ain't God good!" my father, Pastor Richard King shouted to his congregation.

"Yes, he is!" a woman shouted above the rest.

"All the time!" many others shouted as they all clapped.

I sat behind my father on his right side, right next to Deacon Sprite. My father reminded me of the famous T.D. Jakes. Except my father was a skin complexion lighter. My father had the same shape, weight, and grey mustache as the famous Jakes.

My father stood at his pulpit. It was a hand sculpted pulpit my mother got for him for their twentieth anniversary. It was made out of oakwood. It had my father's favorite Bible scripture carved into it at the very front in bold letters. In the very center were the initials of my fathers' first and last name. He still tells people to this day that my mother's alter gift is the best gift he's ever received.

I looked to the side of me as Deacon Sprite nodded off into Lala land. He often nodded off in the middle of my father's sermons. I don't really think the sermons bored, or bothered him, I honestly just think that old age and A/C doesn't mix well together. In the midst of sitting down on a comfortable chair in the A/C, a few Z's will accumulate.

"See, God will hide from you in the midst of the storm, to see if you still have the word, 'Good', in your vocabulary. As some of the true, non-believers seem to forget the true goodness of God, and place him on a fiery throne next to Satan. See, God is good, was good, and always will be, good!" my father said as the crowd applauded him yet again.

That was another reason why I didn't want to take over my father's church. I did in fact know the Bible. I had been raised up on it for as long as I could remember. The thing was, I couldn't talk the Bible like my father could. When it comes to preaching the word of God, my father was the G.O.A.T. He couldn't be topped. It would be impossible for me to fill a set of shoes that's been custom made.

"In the midst of the storm, your storm, you have to look past the clouds, and vision the sun," my father said as he walked from behind his pulpit. He always wore a microphone on his shirt so he could always be heard.

"Now, the reason I said, 'your storm', is because, when it rains on your side of town, it might just be sunny on my side of town. When it snows on your side of town, it might only rain on my side of town. We all go through storms in life, but yours might be over at the snap of a finger, but it might rain over my head for days. Instead of asking God why it always rains on your head, and the sun always shines on sister Dorothy's head, start planting good seeds, brace for the rain, be patient and wait for the sun to come back out. Watch, when God shines his light down on you, you'll be able to sit back and enjoy the fruits."

I looked around as people jumped to their feet clapping as if they had no other use for their hands. My father looked around at his congregation, they were his family. His children. His flock. They looked to him for guidance, and he looked to them for confirmation. They were one in the same, but nothing without each other. I stood to my feet and clapped also. My mother stood in the very front. She had her very own seat, the very first one, right next to sister Dorothy, who was actually the oldest member of the church.

The loud clapping caused Deacon Sprite to stir from his slumber. He began to clap like he knew exactly what everyone was clapping about. I laughed on the inside because even though everyone would see Deacon Sprite asleep during the sermons, no one would ever call him out about it.

The pianist began his slow key as my father descended the stairs. "In life, we have to prepare for storms. We may not see the clouds; we may not hear the thunder, and we may not feel the rain. But that doesn't mean it's not coming. A lot of people will go to the store, and spend thousands on flashlights, batteries, bottled water, and canned goods, just to last through a storm. Some of you might ask yourself, how do I prepare myself for a spiritual storm?" my father said, then paused like most preachers do to get the congregations attention.

"You have to plant good seeds and love your neighbor like you love yourselves. Again, someone might be thinking, 'Preacher, but I do actually plant good seeds. And I do love my neighbors'. Well, I come to you today to tell you that is not all! An important ingredient, you know the one I'm talking about. The secret sauce your mama and grandma put on her pork chops, yeah, that one" my father joked bringing laughter to the room. I had to laugh as well. Lord knows my grandma had a secret sauce that she kept a secret.

"The secret ingredient, is none other than paying your tithes," my father continued. "The Bible says that we should store our treasures up in Heaven. Paying out tithes is the secret ingredient to storing our treasures up in Heaven. Now, you don't have to give your house up, because God already has a mansion in Heaven with your name on it. You just have to have a ticket."

As my father talked to his flock, Deacon Sprite and I walked down the steps and stood behind two separate collection plates. Four ushers went down each row passing along a smaller collection plate to the motherboard of the church and also to the ones that couldn't get up to walk around.

As the ushers finished, they motioned to the back row to stand. Everyone that actually wanted to personally walk to the front was given a chance. My father took tithing time as his time to sing his favorite gospel song. Forgive me Lord for lying, because he couldn't sing one bit. It sounded more like cackling.

"I come from a po' family, we didn't have much, but the Loord... been gooodd... to me," my father sung as people of the congregation paid their tithes. Every time my father sings his favorite song, I always laugh in my head.

See, my father was actually born and raised in Memphis Tennessee. So, when he talks, he talks with his southern accent. So, when he sings his favorite song, it sounds like he's saying 'po', instead or poor when he sings. I swear it never gets old to me.

"God bless you," Sister Martha said to me as she dropped her tithe in the bucket in front of me as she snapped to my father's horrible singing.

I will be honest, and not just because we 're in church. I do love my father's sermons, but his sermons aren't my favorite part about coming to church. My favorite part has to be either tithe time, or when the choir finally sings and all the women gets up to dance and praise the Lord. Again, I have to be honest, I watch those women as they praise the Lord, and on the inside while they're praying whatever they're praying, I'm also praying. As they're praying for whatever it is they're praying for, I'm silently praying that their titties will pop out of their dresses.

I always have to put my hands in my pockets because sometimes my mind gets the best of me. I'll be staring at a woman while she's praising, her hips would be moving to the beat of the drums. God, I swear it would look like I'm at Prospect Park, and Drake is performing with Nicki Minaj the way those women hips would be shaking.

"Any last tithe before we pray our way home?" my father asked. A few stragglers stood to their feet. One was an older lady who was always one of the last people to walk up her tithe. This woman had a fat ass, and she always modeled it in her tight skirts that had a long slit up the back that's normally too high for church. I came to realization that she would always wait until my father called last call so she could be the center of attention. And God did she have my undivided attention. Maybe mine, and every other man in the room.

As everyone's eyes were staring at Sister Fatass, my eyes got diverted to a dark-skinned woman that walked from the back of the room with a ten-dollar bill in her hand. I was glad that Sister Fatass had everyone's attention, or everyone would've noticed how hard I was staring at the beautiful, chocolate queen that stood in front of me. She dropped her money in the bucket, her head was down. She had long dark black hair that came down a little past her shoulders. She looked amazing in her dark blue blouse with the matching skirt to match. She didn't have on the same slutty skirt like Sister Fatass always wore. Hers had class.

"Thank you," I said, causing her to break her deep thought and look up at me. I looked directly in her beautiful brown eyes. Something about her eyes seemed familiar to me, like somehow we had met before and couldn't remember where. As beautiful as she was, I knew if I had met her before, I would always remember.

"What are you thanking me for?" she asked, curiously.

I showed her my signature smile, then said, "For showing me there is a God."

She looked at me in shock. "Wow, hitting on women in church, classic," she said then turned while shaking her head as she walked back to her seat.

The entire way back, I watched her. She had the sexiest pair of smooth legs I've ever seen. But nothing could compare to the ass that popped out of her skirt. I knew God broke the mold when he made her.

Deacon Sprite walked up to me to take the collection plate to be counted. The pianist slowed the tune down so that my father could close out in prayer. Even though he was closing out in prayer, he wouldn't make it home until at least eight or nine tonight. I couldn't tell you one single word my father said as he closed out in prayer. While everyone's eyes were closed, and heads bowed, mines were open. My head was up. I couldn't help myself as I stared at the beautiful chocolate woman in the back.

Xtasy

Chapter 3

I yawned as I stood behind my father as he shook everyone's hand like he was a state senator running for president. My father was a dedicated man. He was dedicated to his marriage, and he was dedicated to his church family. I could honestly say that I was dedicated to one thing in my life like my father. When it came to family, I was one hundred percent committed, and dedicated. On the other hand, I was dedicated to a few other things that my father wouldn't approve of, preferably sex.

Me and sex go wayyy back. Forget four flats on a Cadillac. Me and sex go way back like a Ferrari engine. I couldn't quite put my finger on what it was that got me so addicted, but, wait, me putting my finger on a woman's pussy is what got me addicted in the first place.

Something out of the corner of my eye caught my attention. I turned to the side to see Sister Fatass staring at me. The way she was looking at me made me think of how a fat cop looks at a box of his favorite doughnuts. The gleam in her eyes said she wanted to eat me up. She stared at me while she licked her lips seductively. I looked around to make sure no one saw her. Luckily everyone was too busy waiting in line to shake my father's hand. Sister Fatass walked in my direction, then she turned in the direction of the women's restroom.

I knew what time it was. It was time for Sister Fatass to confess her sins.

After a brief minute or two, I excused myself and made my way down the long hallway. I did a full three sixty to see where Sister Fatass went. I opened the men's restroom and stuck my head inside to look for her. I closed the door back and then I knocked on the ladies room door. I wasn't just going to open the door to see if she was inside. I began to pace as I waited to see if Sister Fatass would come out, or give me the indication that she was inside, and alone, so that I could lay my prayer hands on her head.

Pacing always helped me clear my head. I had to make sure I had a clear head to try and figure out how I was going to handle sister Fatass' fat ass. As I was pacing, trying to come up with a master plan, the financial room door opened. Before I could turn to see who was coming out the room, I was snatched inside.

Sister Fatass planted a juicy kiss on my lips as the door closed. As our kiss broke, she wiped the saliva from the corner of my mouth with her finger. I pretended to be in shock as I imagined the positions I would put her in.

"My God, you look like your father when he was your age. So young, strong, and handsome," she said as she rubbed up and down my right arm. I didn't know if I should've taken her words as a compliment, or an insult. Her saying I look like my father when he was younger only made me think that I would resemble him when I became older. Water or not, that would be a hard pill to swallow.

"Sister Fa-, I mean, Sister Johnson, what are you doing?" I asked, pretending to be shocked.

"Oh, Xzavier, stop it! I see the way you look at me when I walk up and down the aisles. I can feel the way your eyes undress me. You don't have to pretend."

I remained silent. I knew my rights.

"Do you remember when you were a kid? You used to always keep your hands on my big juicy titties," she recalled as she grabbed my hand and brought it to her full chest. I kept my hand as still as possible. I could feel her heartbeat under my hand. Her nipple poked under her bra. It reminded me of an arrow. Sharp at the tip, but fat on the sides. Hard, yet deadly in the wrong hands.

"How's it feel, honey?" she asked. "I know you remember how good they felt," she said as I swallowed the lump in my throat.

"I-It feels, good," I said.

She smiled.

My hand moved slowly around her juicy tit. They were God made. Real, and juicy. I moved my thumb across her hard nipple. A deep breath escaped her mouth.

"Xzavier," she called out with slitted eyes. "Honey, we can only do this one time, and one time only. I know how good dick does a woman my age, so you have to take it easy on me. But we can only do this once. I-I just have to get you out of my system."

By now, my dick is leaking with dick vomit. I may have to talk to Mr. Ralph Lauren himself. Hard-ons aren't made for slacks. I'll have to convince him to come up with a new line. Maybe he could use the name, 'Dick Release' Yeah, sounds like a million-dollar idea.

Sister Johnson grabbed my hard dick through my pants. Her freshly manicured cat claw nails teased the lining of my dick.

"Ahhh, Sister!" I said as her hand made my chest moved up and down.

"We have to hurry," she said as she unzipped my pants and stuck her hand inside without asking.

Sister Johnson wasn't old as she pretended to be as she dropped down in a squat position in front of my hard dick.

"Ohh, God! Look at it. It's beautiful," she said marveled at the size.

I looked up at the ceiling. I had no one else to thank but God. The church had some of the best A/C in the whole city of Houston, but Sister Johnson used her juicy lips to heat my dick up. I knew me and Sister Johnson were both sinning, so I couldn't judge her for her sins. She was a victim of the devil. So, since I couldn't judge her, I couldn't sentence her. I had no choice but to drop her charges of Involuntary dick slaughter.

"God, Sister Johnson. Hell, ain't ready for you," I said with my eyes closed.

Sister Johnson swallowed my dick in a circular motion. There was so much spit on the head of my dick I thought she'd baptized it. I don't know what she was trying to say with my dick in her mouth, but if I had to guess, she was speaking in tongues.

Sister Johnson released my dick from her mouth like a wrongly convicted prisoner. She stood to her feet. She reached behind her back and began to unzip her skirt.

"Sister, wait!" I stopped her. "Leave it on." I smiled mischievously. Sister Johnson smiled as well.

"How do you want me?" She asked. "Bent over the desk, or bent over the couch?"

I looked at my options. The chair looked like a perfect spot to blow her back out on. Then I looked to the desk. All the tithe money from the days service was still in the buckets on the desk waiting for the financial treasury to count and log it. As I looked at the desk, an idea came to mind.

"Bend over the desk," I commanded. Sister Johnson did so with a smile to make the dentist billboard.

I looked at Sister Johnsons backside. As a teen, I had masturbated countless times to Sister Johnsons rump shaker. Now here I was with her bent over the desk, ready for me to part her red sea. I grabbed the helm of her skirt and began to raise it above her thick, juicy thighs. As I got to her round ass, I had to tug the skirt with a little force to get it over her ass cheeks.

Sister Johnson had on a pair of burgundy Victoria Secret panties that was a case of false advertisement. The brand was called Victoria Secret, but the way Sister Johnson's panties were all in her pussy, Victoria revealed it all.

I stared, marveled by all the ass Sister Johnson had stuffed behind her tinted skirt. Sister Johnson had stretch marks peeping from behind her panties. If it was one thing I loved about a thick woman, it was stretch marks and Sister Johnson had a gang of them.

Chill bumps began to show on her caramel ass cheeks as the cold A/C smacked her ass. I rubbed my hand across her ass cheeks like it was the hood of a new car. I tapped the inside of Sister Johnson's thigh. She wasn't new to the game; she was a seasoned vet. Sister Johnson spread her legs to fully assume the position, then she put a dip in her back.

I grabbed my dick and shook it to get the dick vomit to come out. Sister Johnson looked over her shoulder as I stepped closer to her box. As I lined my dick up with her love box, Sister Johnson wiggled her ass at me, enticing me, urging me on. I rubbed the head of my dick up and down her warm slit. Her pussy was fat and juicy. I hadn't even slid into her paradise and yet she had the head of my dick shining like a new marble.

I eased the head past her slit. I held my position to let the heat from her oven thaw me out. Sister Johnson's pussy was so tight, I had to take my time easing past her walls.

"That's it, honey. Fuck mama good." Sister Johnson moaned as I held on to
her hips.

I fucked her from the back as her ass bounced and jiggled against my mid-section. Her pussy juice spilled from between her thighs and soaked my pants.

"Sister Johnson, my God, Sister Johnson!" I panted as I pulled her back and forth onto me.

"Won't he do it!" Sister Johnson said as she reached forward to grab the desk. I was fucking her so hard that I thought for sure someone would hear us. My instincts told me to look and see if the door was locked. And to my amazement, it wasn't.

"Sister Johnson, the door," I said as I kept massaging her insides with my dick.

"Okay, baby," she replied as she spread her ass cheeks. Her. asshole sprouted like a flower bed of roses. She mistakenly thought I wanted her to let me fuck her in her juicy ass.

I knew I had to lock the door, but the feeling of her juicy walls clamping down on my dick wouldn't let me pull out. Sister Johnson accidently knocked over the the buckets, spilling loose bills and coins all over the desk.

I reached over her and grabbed a handful of bills. I threw them over her head making it rain without missing a single stroke. The money fell all over her body. Ben Franklin landed on her sticky ass and stayed there. I smacked her ass right beside Ben Franklin's face.

"Mama's cumming!" Sister Johnson moaned. I placed my hand over her mouth as I fucked her harder. Her moans turned into small cries as our bodies rocked the desk from side to side. I looked down to see the front of my pants soaked with her juices.

I used my right hand to grip her shoulder as my left hand clasped around her mouth. My balls began to swell as my dick got harder. Hot cum shot out of my hard dick into Sister Johnson's already soaked pussy. I wasn't worried about her getting pregnant. I was sure her baby days were long behind her. Sister Johnsons legs wobbled as she passed out over the desk. I pushed my dick inside of her pussy until I was balls deep. I stayed still, enjoying the warm feeling. She had already told me that we would never be able to have sex again, so I had to hold on to the sensual feeling for as long as she would allow me.

"Sister Johnson, that was amazing," I said as I pulled my sticky dick from her pussy. I took a step back to give her space to pull her skirt down. She stayed in the same position, bent over the desk with her Victoria Secret panties pulled to the side.

My head jerked to the side as I heard the sound of the doorknob moving from the outside. Sister Johnson heard the sound too as she tried to rush to fix her clothes. I stuffed my semi-hard dick in my boxers and zipped my pants just as the door opened.

Chapter 4
Sonja

Church was my safe haven. The place I went to find peace and comfort.

I was new to the city of Houston, so I didn't have a church family as of yet. I heard from mutual friends that the Lord's Manna was the church to attend while you were in Houston Texas. And I have to admit, the service today left me feeling so much better than how I came.

See, I was forced to move from my hometown, Waco Texas, to Southwest Houston because my husband, Donnie Echols opened up a night club in Southwest Houston. Donnie is actually from the 5th Ward section of Houston. Donnie came to Waco one day to look for some new talent to bring to his city, but the famous local rapper Hotboy Wes ended up getting signed by Gucci Mane's 1017 label.

Donnie set his eyes back on going to Houston. As he stopped at the gas station, he noticed me at the pump pumping gas. I was fresh out of 24 Hour Fitness. My spandex was skintight, all up my coochie. My hair was pulled back in a ponytail. It was frizzy, but I still looked good.

Donnie walked up to me with his thuggish, yet corporate swagger. I can still remember the sweet words he said to grasp my attention.

"I don't care how high gas gets, as long as I know there's beautiful women like you here, I'll spend my last dime for a full tank."

I will admit, it was kinda corny, but it made me laugh, especially since gas prices had sky-rocketed to almost five dollars a gallon. After that day at the gas station, me and Donnie saw each other on a regular basis. Donnie spent so much time in Waco with me that he had to get a condo. It wasn't long before Donnie abandoned his condo to move in with me, and shortly after that, we were walking down the aisle in holy matrimony. We said our vows in Waco, Texas on my Uncle Williams fifteen-acre farm surrounded by all of my family. My wedding present from Donnie was a trip to Paris, and a new house built from the ground up in Houston. I will say, my life turned out great. I have a very handsome husband who's very wealthy, smart, and ambitious who loves and adores me.

I know, everyone has a 'but' somewhere tucked deep in their closet. I know I said all of those precious things about my husband, and they're all true. But there is one thing that I wish I could change about my marriage. Don't get me wrong, Donnie isn't an unfaithful, or abusive husband. He's very faithful and caring! In fact, I don't think any woman would want to cheat with his shrimp dick tail.

Yup, I said it! My loving, rich, sexy husband has a small, shrimp dick. And it's not a fresh jumbo shrimp either. It's one of those pop-corn shrimp ones. Okay, maybe it's a little bigger, but you get my point. My husband was everything a woman wanted emotionally, and financially, but when it came to the bedroom, he was in last place.

Over the course of our marriage, we've survived off of love alone. I can't say that I don't get sexually frustrated, because I do. And I mean really frustrated. There be times when my pussy is on fire, I mean I be so wet and anxious to cum, but my husband's dick isn't big enough to bring me to climax.

Even though since we've said 'I do', I've been extremely hot and bothered, I still remain faithful to my husband. For better, or for worse, right?

That's really the reason I had to go to church. Lately, I've been having the urge to cure the itch that's been driving my pussy crazy. I'm not a cheater. Never have, never will. But somewhere along the line of being faithful, infidelity planted a seed in my mind. And I've tried hard not to water it, because I was afraid of what would come of it. But now, I needed help. I needed Jesus.

Pastor Richard King's sermon today made me feel a little better. He didn't actually speak on my husband's small penis, but he did speak on planting seeds and outlasting storms. I felt like God was speaking through Pastor Richard King directly to me in some odd way. When it was time to pay our tithe, I took a ten-dollar bill from my wallet and stood up to walk it to the front of the church. Maybe in my mind I was trying to buy an answered prayer from God. Lord knows I could use one.

In the midst of paying my tithe, I began to say a prayer in my mind. My prayer was interrupted by an usher standing in front of a tithe bucket.

"Thank you," he said, causing me to look up at him. As I looked at him, he stared directly in my eyes.

"What are you thanking me for?" I asked curiously.

The man before me smiled, then said, "For showing me there is a God."

When I tell you I was baffled by his comment, that would be an understatement. I had to keep it cordial being that we were in the house of the Lord. "Wow, hitting on women in church, classic." I turned and walked away as I shook my head. I knew he was staring at my ass as I was walking away, I could practically feel his eyes burning a hole through my panties.

As I took my seat in the back of the church, I looked to the very front at the man that had used his best pickup line on me. And honestly, this was weird, but I couldn't help but smile and shake my head. It was the first time a man has pushed up on me at church. Wait, except for when Donnie's Uncle Ralph tried to feel up on me on my wedding day, but that doesn't really count.

Pastor King began to pray the service out, so I bowed my head. I prayed as Pastor King prayed. I prayed for a lot of things too. I prayed for a secure marriage. I prayed that I could remain faithful, and I prayed that God would add a few inches to Donnie's' penis. I know I'm dead wrong, but being married to a man with a small penis was already killing me softly.

After Pastor King finished praying, I grabbed my purse and headed to the front of the church to have a few words with Pastor King. I had to wait in line as it seemed like the entire congregation wanted to shake his hand.

"Hello sister, I pray that you enjoyed the sermon today," Pastor King said as he pulled me in for a hug.

"In fact, Pastor King, I did. And the choir, my God they are blessed with voices of angels," I complimented.

"They do show out, huh." he smiled. "Do you sing any, Ms.—?"

"Oh, I'm sorry. My name is Sonja Echols. And yes pastor, I sing, dance. I'll do anything for the Lord."

"Really, well we were thinking about starting a praise dance team, but we didn't have any dance instructors. If you're int—"

"I'll be honored," I said cutting him off.

"My son, Xzavier is right over there. Let him know I sent you and he'll set you up with everything you'll need," Pastor King said pointing.

I looked at the man the Pastor was pointing at. It just so happened to be the exact same man that had tried his luck only minutes before.

"Thank you, Pastor King," I said as I looked at his son from a distance.

Xzavier was already headed in a different direction. I took a brief moment to decide on if I wanted to wait on him to come back or go behind him.

Oh well, I figured I might as well go after him. By the time I made it down the hallway, Xzavier was nowhere in sight. I stood in the hallway as I patiently waited on him to come out of the men's room. Then, I looked around and saw that there were three other doors he could've went into. There was the financial room, the Pastor's office, and the ladies room. I was going to automatically cancel the thought of him being in the ladies room, then I remembered how he tried to shoot his shot at me while I was paying my tithes.

After waiting what felt like forever for Xzavier to come out of the restroom, I came to my senses that maybe he wasn't there. So, my next thought was the Pastor's office. I began to walk past the financial room. What sounded like a woman's moan caused me to stop in my tracks.

I back tracked and stood perfectly still outside the door. I thought my mind and ears were playing tricks on me. I could've sworn I heard a woman's voice say, 'Mama's cumming'. I could've been hearing things, but for a woman who watches porn six times a week, I know the sound of skin slapping skin.

I had to cover my mouth to prevent myself from bursting out in laughter.

I couldn't point out who it was, but if I had to guess, I would say it was Xzavier. Just the thought of his mannish, cute, dark, handsome self beating a woman's guts in really turned me on. It had been just last week since me and my husband Donnie had sex, but it's been since high school, my senior year to be exact since I last had an orgasm. By the sounds on the other side of the door, whoever the man was knew exactly what he was doing.

My inner slut kicked in. My mind was telling me to mind my own business and walk away. But the moisture between my thighs convinced me otherwise.

All I really wanted was to get a sneak peek. I only wanted to know if it was Xzavier or not.

I placed my hand on the doorknob and froze. I was tryna be as sneaky as possible. I couldn't believe my lack of sex had turned me into a peeping tom. I turned the doorknob while listening for the faint sound. I listened closely. I couldn't hear a sound. And that's when I realized that I'd gave myself up.

I opened the door pretending that my intentions weren't to eavesdrop. I looked around as Xzavier looked at me in shock. There was a woman inside who was pretty. Off the bat, I could tell that she was up in age. She wore a very tight skirt that made her ass look like a beach ball. She stood frozen like a statue. Xzavier cleared his throat as he stared at me.

I looked around the room. There were crumbled up bills all over the desk and floor. Xzavier's eyes followed mines. He stuck his hands in his pockets then said, "Sister Johnson, thank you for assisting me with counting up todays tithing." Sister Johnson looked at Xzavier, then she nodded as she cleared her throat.

"Oh, no problem. You know I'll do anything to help the church," she said as she looked at her smart watch. "I have to get going now, I still have to get Sunday dinner ready for my grandkids." She hugged Xzavier before she hurriedly walked out the door.

Xzavier looked at me, then he let out an embarrassing laugh. "Were you looking for the ladies room? If so, it's actually the door on the right," he said as he began to pick up loose bills and coins that were scattered around.

I tried hard not to laugh. Xzavier tried to clean up the mess he made, but he couldn't do anything to mask the strong smell of sex in the air.

"No, actually I was looking for you," I said.

"Don't mean to sound rude," he said. "But why were you looking for me?" he asked. As hard as he tried not to sound rude or angry, he did. I knew the reason why. I had barged in on his fuck session.

"I'm new here," I started to shake his hand, but only God knows exactly where they've been. Well, God and Sister Johnson. "I spoke with your father, Pastor King. He wanted me to help with the praise dance team," I explained.

"But we don't have a praise dance team," he replied.

"I know. He spoke on starting one," I said.

Xzavier nodded as he walked around the desk and sat in the brown leather chair. "What's your name?" he asked.

"Sonja Echols."

"You already know my name, but I will properly introduce myself," he said as he pulled a bottle of hand sanitizer from the desk drawer and squirted some onto his hands, then he rubbed them together.

He stood up with his hands stretched out to me. "I'm Xzavier Cornelious King. As of now, I'm the head of the Deacon board. And soon to be head Pastor of the Lords Manna."

I smiled on the outside as I shook his hand. I smiled on the outside, but on the inside I almost died. It was only seconds ago that Xzavier was banging Sister Johnson's back out, and now he stood before me speaking as if he was a saint without a spot or a blemish.

I played along. "It's a pleasure to meet you. Wait! You're the one that I helped realize that God is real, right?" I laughed.

Xzavier laughed as well. "I guess you're right," he said as he walked from behind the desk and sat on the very edge. His dick rested on the side of his leg. His dick print showed clear as day. I had to look away to prevent from staring. Other than my every night occasion with porn, I hadn't seen a man's dick in years.

"So, Sonja. Where are you from?" He asked as he looked at my ring finger.

I never wore my wedding ring for my own reasons. I could tell me not having on a ring was the reason for Xzavier's smile.

"I'm from Waco Texas," I answered.

"Country girl, huh." he smiled. "So, what bring you to the big city?"

"Uhm jobs, I guess. Waco doesn't really have any good paying jobs. I guess me being from Waco, I got tired of doing the same ol' things every day."

He licked his lips slowly, then asked. "What kind of things do you like to do?"

I kept a straight face even though I knew his question was a loaded one.

"I, uh—I enjoy working out, I'm a personal trainer. I'm also a dancer."

His right eyebrow raised in suspicion. "That's exotic, I-I mean, that's good. A personal trainer, and a dancer. What kind of dancing do you do?"

Typical man. All he really heard out of everything I said, was that I was a dancer. He didn't give a damn that I said I was a personal trainer. I already knew he was displaying images in his mind of me sliding up and down a stripper pole. I wouldn't be surprised if he was having images of me sliding up and down his pole. He had this big cheesy smile on his face, and a gleam of lust
in his eyes.

"Uhm, all kinds actually. I do Salsa, I Tango, and I do praise dance."

Xzavier smiled. "I did a little tango back in my college days."

"Really," I said, surprised.

"You say that like you don't believe me," he said.

"I just didn't take you as a man that tangos. Normally when someone grows up in the church, all he or she knows is the word of God," I explained.

He smiled. "You 're right about that. I was raised up in the church, and I do know a lot about God, but that's not all I know of. I can show you a few things, if you're interested. Tango, that is," he said cleaning it up quickly.

Xzavier wasn't shy in his approach. I could tell that he did this all the time. "Uhm, I don't think that's a good idea," I said.

"Why not? It won't be like a date or anything. We could just go out to dance, and also discuss the possibility of you starting a praise dance team. Unless you have a boyfriend or something that won't approve of us going out?"

I couldn't believe him. Here he was, asking me out, with a dirty, sticky dick laying on his leg. He didn't even have the audacity to clean himself off first. Men!

"It's not that I have a boyfriend or anything like that. It's just that I don't want people to see us out, you know, people of the church, and get the wrong idea. I don't want to ruin your image. You're next in line for the pulpit. That's something to think about."

Xzavier nodded. "I guess you're right." He stood up and stared at me. "But, if you ever change your mind, let me know. I've never been the one to care what people think of me. Let them talk, but in the end, there's only one true judge."

I nodded. "You're absolutely correct about that. But I have to go now. I guess I'll be seeing you around." I turned and placed my hand on the doorknob. I took my time turning it. If there was one thing a man was soft behind, was a woman with a nice behind.

"Uhm, Ms. Echols," Xzavier said as he walked behind me. I turned to see what he wanted.

"Can you come by the church tomorrow? We'll discuss the praise dance team here. That way you'll feel more comfortable."

I smiled and nodded. "That would be great. I'll see you tomorrow." I turned again and this time walked out the room. I could hear Xzavier behind me. He stopped in the doorway and watched me walk away. I knew the entire time he watched my ass sway left to right. I smiled as I turned the corner. This was going to be like taking candy from a baby.

Chapter 5
Sonja

"Babe, where are you!" I yelled out loud as I walked into the mini mansion that my husband Donnie got built from the ground up for me. I laid my purse down on the side table by the door and placed my keys in the glass dish.

Something smelled delicious as I walked through the house to get to the kitchen. I smiled as I placed my hands on my hips. My husband Donnie had his wireless Beats headphones in his ear as he danced back and forth with his back to me. He was wearing an apron, the one I bought for him. It had the words King of The Kitchen written on the front in red and gold letters. Donnie was shirtless and his masculine arms were on public display. That was another reason why I fell for Donnie. Donnie was athletic like me. We both enjoyed working out. We decided to have an indoor gym for both of our pleasure of staying in shape. Donnie was a weights kind of guy. He loved the bench press. And I loved that he loved it. His arms were so big and cut. It brought out his shoulders.

I leaned against the counter as I watched Donnie dance to whatever song he was listening to. It was then that Donnie started mumbling on certain parts that I realized that he was listening to Return of The Mack by Mark Morrison.

"You lied to me, all these pains you said I'll never feel!" Donnie sung as loud as he could. He opened the oven and bent over to grab whatever it was he had cooked. I took that as my chance to sneak up on him. I crept behind him, being as quiet as possible. With his loud singing, I could've been as loud as I wanted to be, I don't think he would've heard me either way.

As Donnie bent over, I slapped him on his ass, startling him. He held on to the pan of baked chicken as he jumped back startled. He sat the pan on the stove as he took one of his earbuds out of his ear.

"Sonja, babe! You could've got hurt creeping up on me like that," he said.

I laughed hard at his statement. "Oh really, and what would you have done, feed me to death." I laughed, toying with him.

He laughed also. "Oh, you think that's funny, huh?" he said as he grabbed me, picked me up, and sat me on the countertop.

Donnie kissed me ever so passionately as he took his oven mitts off and tossed them on the counter beside the chicken. As we kissed, I ran my soft hands across Donnie's perfectly shaved head. We kissed what seemed like minutes. The moisture between my sex lips were evidence enough to know that I was turned on. Donnie stepped back and looked at me.

"Damn woman, you come home straight from church feeling freaky. What did the preacher preach about that got you so aroused?" Donnie asked.

I placed my hand between my legs to calm myself down. It wasn't the sermon that got me aroused. It was the preacher's son that got me so hot and bothered. But I couldn't tell Donnie that. "Stop it, babe. The sermon was good, but that's not what got me feeling like this. I can't come home to find my ever so handsome husband in the kitchen cooking me a meal and decide to skip straight to dessert."

Donnie pulled me to the edge of the counter and kissed my lips. Our tongues tackled each other's as they wrestled back and forth. As we broke our kiss, Donnie looked into my eyes as he pulled my skirt above my box. My laced Victoria Secret panties were soaked in the front from my arousal. Donnie bit the crotch area of my panties. His teeth felt good on my pussy as I leaned my head back in pleasure. If it was one thing Donnie was good at, it was eating pussy.

I mean he had to be good at it, considering his dick game was beyond terrible.

Donnie bent his knees a tad. He held my legs open with his right arm, while he kept my skirt raised with his left hand. My head touched the cabinet as Donnie snatched my panties to the side. My pussy was glistening like it was sweating. I was beyond horny. I couldn't stop having thoughts of Xzavier penetrating my pussy in the financial room like he did Sister Johnson. It had been so long since I've had sex that it hurt.

Donnie inserted two of his fingers in my tight hole, just the feel of his fingers deep in my hole caused me to gasp. Donnie worked his fingers in and out of my slippery hole as I gripped the edge of the sink for support. I felt his hot breath as he leaned closer to my box. He licked my swollen pearl as he worked his fingers in my hole. His tongue moved at a fast pace as his tongue swiped over and back on my clit. I gripped his head for support, the edge of the counter had got slippery from my sweaty hands. Donnie tried to move his tongue from my clit, but I wasn't having it. I smushed his face into my box, force feeding him. He didn't deny me, but his eyes looked up at mine as I humped into his mouth.

"Don't stop, bae. That's it right there. Make me cum, please," I begged as I humped into his mouth.

Donnie worked his fingers faster and faster into my box as I felt myself about to cum. I had to get mine first, because I knew Donnie would want to get his second. And once he got inside of me, the mood would be off. And I mean completely off.

Donnie pressed his tongue flat on my clit as he mushed it back and forth while humming God knows what. The feeling was exquisite. I mean it's so hard to describe. In a sense, I felt like I was cheating on my husband. While he was eating my pussy, I was imagining it was another man doing it. While he was pumping my pussy with his fingers, I was imagining it was Xzavier's, but bigger.

"You like that?" Donnie asked as he continued to eat my box.

I nodded, wishing he would just stay quiet so I could keep my fantasy going without him interrupting it.

"Say you like the way I eat this pussy," he said as he slurped on my juices. I closed my eyes tight as I tried to get Donnie's face out of my mind and put Xzavier's there. I knew if I kept ignoring Donnie, he wouldn't stop talking until I finally answered him. He was the verbal kind of lover; he just had to talk and get a response.

"Yes, daddy. It feelsss sooo gooood," I said just to get him to shut up. I wasn't lying, the feeling was amazing. He knew exactly how to work his tongue. The only thing was he never knew how to tame it.

Donnie pressed his tongue on my clit harder as he continued to hum. His tongue felt like a human vibrator. His fingers hooked inside of my hole as he scraped my walls with them bringing me over the top to my climax. My body began to shake as it let out my lustful sins.

Donnie stood up and untied his string to his sweatpants as they fell to the ground. Under his sweatpants, he wore a pair of tight Gucci boxer briefs that hugged his dick. He wore them to make his penis look bigger than what it was. Donnie took ahold of his small penis and began to slow stroke it using just two fingers. His thumb was on the top side of his dick, and his pointer finger was under it doing its best to bring it to life.

Donnie stared into my eyes as he tried to get his dick hard. I kept my legs open wide so he could see my juices seeping from my box. The quicker he got off, the quicker I could go take a shower and clear my mind. Donnie wasn't a quick pumper at all. He could go for hours, the only thing, I would forget he would be inside of me.

"Get it hard for me, daddy," I urged him on. I wanted him to at least get himself halfway off, so when he finally penetrates me, he would at least be halfway finished.

Donnie looked deep into my pussy as he stroked his dick. He grunted deep in his throat as he raised up on his tiptoe. I could sense he was feeling the motion and the girth of his hand because his eyes began to close as he slowly walked up to me. I scooted to the edge of the counter and opened my legs as far as they would open. Donnie reached out to me. I grabbed his right arm and held on to it. He leaned over me and placed his dick at my center.

"You ready, babe?" he asked as he opened his eyes and looked at me. He always asked me that before he stuck his dick in me, like his size would actually hurt me. I guess it was my fault. All those years of fake screaming and yelling like his size was actually punishing my pussy.

I nodded as I bit my bottom lip. As he pushed his head inside of me, I held my breath and gasped as if I was a virgin all over again. I knew it always turned him on even more when I did it.

"Oh, babe!" I yelled as I placed my hand at the base of his stomach. Donnie rocked back and forth into me as he kept slipping out.

"Fuck me babe, harder." I moaned as I closed my eyes. I bit into my lip to prevent myself from laughing.

Donnie grabbed me around the back of my neck and pulled me closer to him. I could feel his dick inside of me as he fucked me harder and harder. Sweat fell from his chest onto me as he continued to buck into me. I looked up at him with bittersweet eyes. I loved that man to death. He was my soulmate, my husband. But he was a terrible lover.

Xtasy

Chapter 6
Xzavier

After I cleaned up the financial office, I documented today's tithing and locked up for the night. As I walked out the room and locked the door, I looked towards my father's office. His door was wide open. He sat in his big leather chair, his glasses laid on the bridge of his nose as he looked at his desk at something important. I quietly placed the keys in my pocket as I tried to sneak away. I had a date tonight, and if my father was to see me, he would hold me up until the sun came up.

I quietly tried to sneak down the hallway. It was like my father had a motion sensor on his glasses because he instantly spotted me. "Xzavier, you all done with the tithes?" he asked. I stood still with my back to him like I was invisible.

I could hear him place his glasses on his desk.

"Xzavier," he called after me again. I guess I wasn't invisible after all.

I turned to him. "Yes, father. I'm all done in there. Everything is all logged and put up in the safe."

"Good, good," he said as he looked at me. "Well, I need you to come and help me with something real quick. That's if you weren't planning on doing anything?" he asked.

I sighed silently so he wouldn't hear me. Of course, I had plans of my own, it was a beautiful Sunday night, the air was breezy, and the stars were out. Who doesn't have plans? But, like a good obedient young man, I walked over in my father's office and said, "I'll help you with whatever you need help with."

"Oh Xzavier, now if you had plans, go out and enjoy yourself, I can handle it."

He said it, but I felt like it was a trick. I walked around his desk and stood beside him. I looked at his desk and looked at a handwritten paper that was laid flat on his desk. It was his hand written, I could tell by all the scribbles and words scratched out. It was a sermon he was working on, probably for the next Sunday.

"Dad, I'm here. What do you need help with?" I asked.

He smiled and patted me on my arm. "I was working on next Sunday's sermon and I kinda got stuck," he said as he picked up the paper and held it out for me.

I grabbed the paper and started from the beginning. It was entitled, 'What Is Done In The Dark'. I started to read from the beginning. I read through the first two paragraphs then I stopped to look at my father. He didn't see me looking at him because he was too busy staring off into space, probably trying to gather his thoughts together to finish what he'd started. The passage was about people doing things in plain sight for everyone to see, then going home to live a life in the darkness. He touched subjects on illegal activities, sex without marriage, homosexuality, sinning pulpits, and even infidelity.

The man said more than a mouthful all in one passage. I nodded my head as I finished reading it, then I handed it back to him. "That's, that's great pops. I don't see what you need help with, you hit every subject right on the nail."

"I-I don't know. It felt like something was missing. I prayed and asked God to make sure he spoke through me, and that's exactly what came to my mind. Yet, somethings not right. I can feel it, like something being left out."

I shook my head. "It all sounds great to me, but you still have at least four more days. I mean its only still Sunday," I said laughing.

My father laughed also. "You're right." he looked up at me and smiled. "You're going to be a great preacher someday, you know that."

I nodded. I didn't want to lie to him, so I just stayed silent. He patted my arm again. "Well, get out of here, go do whatever it was you young kids do these days after church."

I nodded as I looked down at his paper again. He had prayed to God to speak to him before he let his pen do the work of God. If God was telling him to say those things, and then my father all of a sudden asks me to help him with it, somehow God maybe was using him to get through to me. So, I thought. Nah, I'm tripping! God knows my heart. He knows what I'm going to do before I even do it. So, if he knows all of that, then he knew no matter what sign he sent my way, the plans I had for tonight will remain.

"X, what you think?" Rudy, our church's choir director asked me as he yelled above the loud rap music.

Rudy was my best friend. We had been joined at the hip since middle school.

We didn't actually go to the same school, but we did attend the same Sunday school service, my mom and his mom being the teachers. Rudy was light skinned. Very high yellow if he hasn't been in the sun for a while. He had short wavy hair with a taper fade. Despite him once having long dreads, he still had some good hair.

Rudy was from the land of dread heads. He was born and raised from New Orleans, Louisiana. He migrated from New Orleans when Hurricane Katrina hit his hometown. His mother thought that Houston would be a great place to start over, so she changed her scenery for good and called Houston her home.

Rudy and I instantly clicked tight when we first met. We had something in common, girls. During Sunday school, neither of us could keep our eyes, or our hands to ourselves. He was very specific with his choices, only having eyes for light skinned chicks. Me on the other hand, I liked my women like I liked my candy. Didn't matter to me much, I'd stick my hand in the bowl, and come out with something sweet either way. My mother, and his became best friends through their passion and faithfulness to God. My mother and Mrs. Jackson both shared Sunday school and Wednesday Bible school together. They even did majority of their holidays together. With Mrs. Jackson and my mother spending so much time together, it only brought me and Rudy closer together.

It was my mother's idea to start a junior choir for kids. And it was Mrs. Jackson's idea to have her son Rudy join the choir. We were both around the same age then, if I can recall right, maybe eleven or twelve at the time. And I will admit, Rudy had a voice for his age. He used to sing to all the girls in Sunday and gospel wasn't on the playlist. Rudy had a voice like the singer Lyfe Jennings. He had soul. His voice came off as a little raspy, but the boy could blow. Rudy became the face and lead singer of the youth choir. It wasn't long before he graduated to the main choir and it only was a year later that he became the lead singer. At the age of eighteen, he took over as the choir's director, which is a very big thing for a church as big as ours. Rudy wasn't liked much by a lot of people, preferably the men's choirs. Some felt that Rudy hadn't earned the position he was given. Some felt that the reason he was given the position was because of who his mother was, and because his mother and mine were best friends. If you would ask me, I would probably agree with them, but then again, no one could deny the boys talent for music. Rudy won numerous gospel competitions for our church, and he was finally about to record his first gospel album. I was glad to be called his friend.

I looked at the two women he had sitting beside him in the black leather booth and smiled. Rudy had his arm around the light skinned one, so I already saw that he was marking his territory. I gradually walked up to the table. A beautiful brown skinned woman looked up at me. She wore her hair in a long ponytail with a single braid on the side. She wore a beautiful smile. I couldn't deny a woman with a beautiful smile. It was just something about it.

"X, this is Monica, the one that I told you about," Rudy said.
I nodded with a smile. Rudy did in fact tell me about Monica. He had told me during a game of one-on-one basketball that Monica was fine as hell with a beautiful smile. He also told me about the woman he was with, Ria. Ria and Monica were both gospel singers looking to cut a gospel album. Ria and Rudy met at a gospel seminar; she recognized him as he stood up to clap. The way he told me the story, she came on to him, but I know my guy. He thinks, if she grins, she's in. To make a long story short, they exchanged numbers and talked frequently. She agreed to go out with him, but insisted on him bringing a friend to tag along for a double date. When Rudy described Monica to me, and told me that she wanted to go out with me, I had to take him up on his offer. And I thank God that I did. I held my right hand out at Monica.
"Monica, right?" I said with a smile.

Monica smiled and nodded as she held her hand out to shake mines. She sat at the corner seat, so it made it easy for me to pull her up from her seat and hug her. My arm went around her waist as I hugged her.

"It's a pleasure to meet you, Monica," I said as I let her go.

Monica blushed as she looked back at her friend Ria. Ria nodded in approval and smiled back at her.

Monica reclaimed her seat, and I sat down beside her. "Glad that you could make it," Rudy said as he wrapped his arms around Ria.

"You know I couldn't leave you high and dry. I'm always here for you when you need me," I said.

"So, Xzavier," Ria said as she looked at me. "Rudy tells us that you're going to be the next preacher to take the podium at the Lord's Manna. Is that true?"

I smiled as I looked at Monica. "Uhm, I've heard the rumors also," I said then laughed.

"Rumors, huh," Ria replied with a laugh of her own. "I find it very interesting for a man to preach the word of God with such fashion and finesse. You do have some big shoes to fill though. I've heard quite a few sermons from your father. He's one of the greats."

I nodded. "That I can agree with. He's amazing. I, uh. I will say that whenever the day comes for me to preach the word, I will do my best to do it in the manner of my father."

"Do you plan on doing anything different with the church?" Monica asked.

"Like, what?" I asked.

"For instance, your father kinda, how would you say it, uhm. He has and old school style of doing things. A southern style."

"We are in the south, aren't we?" Rudy asked.

"No, I mean like, he has a country style of preaching. His sermons get the message across, but he does in fact have a very large church, with a lot of followers. His sermons are broadcasted all across the world. What I'm trying to say is, now-a-days, in order to get your message across to the younger crowd, you'll have to be more, how would you say it, hip?"

I nodded. "I understand what you're getting at Monica. My father is old school. He preaches the way his father preached."

"So, you're going to preach the way your father preached?" Ria asked.

I sat quietly for a second. In actuality, I didn't plan on preaching at all. But I knew I couldn't tell them that. I had never even told Rudy that I didn't plan on taking over my father's church. Rudy was my boy. My day one. But everyone knew Rudy couldn't keep a secret. At least not one like that.

I sighed. As I was about to answer Ria's question, Rudy said. "Ladies, let's give the man a break with all the questions. At least let the man get the chance to get acquainted with his date first."

I gave Rudy a nod. That was why he was my day one. I didn't have to tell him to throw me a life raft, he could automatically see the despair on my face.

I grabbed the empty glass that was in front of me and filled it with some lemon water from the pitcher in front of me. I placed my lips to the glass and peeped out the corner of my eye at Monica. I couldn't help but wonder what kind of woman she was. I already knew that she was a church going woman. She was a gospel singer. A good one at that. But deep down inside of me, I wondered did she live and died by the word of God. Or did she have a sinful side to her like me. I knew no one was perfect, at least I knew I wasn't.

I took a sip from my glass then sat it down. "So, Monica, tell me about yourself."

She slightly turned to face me giving me a beautiful smile. "Well, what do you want to know?" she asked.

"Tell me somethin' about yourself that you wished you could hide from God?" I asked looking dep into her eyes.

Her friend Ria smiled and nodded. "That's very deep," Ria said as she looked as she was thinking of what her answer would be if she was asked the same question.

"Uhm, I don't know. That's a question I wasn't prepared for," Monica said as she thought hard about the question. "How about you tell me your answer first."

I nodded. I was prepared for her to counter my question. "Let's see, uhm. I believe in God with every bone in my body, yet I wish that sometimes he would turn a blind eye to me so that I could do some of the things that my body craves."

Monica looked at me in shock. Ria smiled as she stared at me. "If you don't mind me asking, what does your body crave?" Ria asked. Monica looked at Ria suspiciously. If I was reading her mind right, she was most likely wondering why Ria would ask me a question like that.

"Sometimes my body craves freedom, like it's being held in a prison with a million guards watching, and a warden looking over them. Like it's being held for a life sentence being someone it doesn't want to be. Sometimes my body craves a passion that God can't satisfy. Sometimes it lusts to the point to where I wish I could sin and not be judged. But then again, my flesh gets the best of me, and I do. I sin, and it feels good, so good that I wish I could live as only my flesh and hide from the principles of the Bible. Then, I wake up, and I'm back being the son of a preacher. The one to take over the pulpit," I said as I looked around in everyone's eyes, reading their thoughts as if they were my own.

"Honesty at its best," Monica said as she looked at me wondering who was the man Rudy had set her up with for a blind date. For a second, I thought that she would get up and walk away without looking back. She didn't. She looked deep into my eyes and said, "Sometimes, as I'm singing gospel music, I wish that I could sing R&B without people judging me, without people calling it the devils music. I often come to church listening to gospel, but once I leave the church parking lot, I change the station to R&B."

"Is there something wrong with you wanting something that you can't have?" I asked her.

"It shouldn't be," she replied.

"So, why do you feel like it's wrong?" I asked.

Monica shrugged. "Because of what people in church says."

"You know, Malcolm X once said, 'I would've been a Christian, if it wasn't for most Christians." What he meant by that was, as Christians, we often over judge each other because of the word of God. But then again, the Bible says to judge not, right?"

Monica nodded.

"Just because a specific group of people says something is wrong, or that you shouldn't have it, that doesn't mean that you shouldn't wish you should have it," I explained.

"If you could have anything right now, at this moment, what would it be?" Monica asked.

"If I tell you that, you'll judge me just like the rest."

"I've been a lot of things in my lifetime. I've dressed up in a lot of costumes for Halloween, but I've never pretended to be God," she said.

"Okay," I said as I looked directly at her. I stayed silent as I bathed in her smile. She was beautiful. Her lips were soft looking, pink, and succulent. Her red lips stick looked as if she had it done by a professional makeup artist. Her hair was short, like a bob style. It was dark black, perfect for her brown eyes. I looked into them, wondering if she would actually judge me for what I was thinking. Lord knows one of my favorite Bible quotes was, 'So is a man thinketh, so is he'. And I was thinking of nothing but passionate sex with her.

"At this very moment, if I could have anything in the world, it would be to dig deep into your mind, into your heart, and dig up that one fantasy of yours that you wish you could have without people judging you."

I looked at Monica as she crossed her brown legs. She placed her right hand on the table and peeped at Ria. Rudy stared at me with a slight grin. Even he was at loss for words.

"If you could read minds, what do you think my fantasy would be?" Monica asked as she looked directly into my eyes.

I smiled. Women were amazing. If only they knew that they really ruled the world. They had one weakness that they couldn't control, it's like their kryptonite. Women had a soft heart, and they wore it on their sleeve. That's what made me so good at what I did. Maybe that's why people always say women could never make it as being the president. They were too emotional. Maybe it's just me, but I read them like an open book.

"Honestly, and this is just what I think your fantasy is. I think, that you want to make a number one R&B album, and make love to it."

Rudy laughed out loud. I looked at him wondering what was funny. "Come on bro, I don't think that's it." Rudy laughed.

I looked at Monica. She stared at me. She wore this gleam in her eye. Like she wanted to let the tear fall that she was holding captive in her eye. "It's crazy that you would say that, Rudy. Because he's right," Monica said as she hung her head in embarrassment.

"If I'm right, then why are you hanging your head?" I asked.

"Because since I've been knowing my voice was so powerful, all I've ever wanted was for people to dance to the sound of my voice. Move their hips to the sweet melody of my words, but my mother raised me in the church, she never allowed me to listen to any other kind of music. Since a kid, I always would sneak and buy different genres of CDs and hide under my bed and listen to them on my CD player. I used to close my eyes, and imagine myself singing in front of a sold-out crowd. The room is dark, and everyone has their phones out. The light from their phones lighting up the room. Lighters flickering in the night. People's bodies swaying from side to side as I sing my heart out. It's weird."

Rudy's jaw dropped as he looked at me. Ria stared at me in awe. I picked my glass up and took another slow sip. A waiter walked up to the table with four menus, stealing the moment. She sat one in front of me, then she walked around the table, placing one in front of each of them. "Hello, I am your waiter for the night. My name is Emily. I would first like to start everyone off with drinks, if that's okay? Then, I'll take your orders." Our waitress was Caucasian. She had a short bobbed styled haircut. It made her neck look long and firm.

Everyone seemed to be still staring at me as the waiter spoke. The stares caused Emily to look at me, too. I took another sip from the glass, smiling behind it. Me taking over a pulpit, yeah right!

As I walked in my two-bedroom house, I closed the front door and locked it behind myself. I watched Monica as her fine ass nervously moved in front of me. She looked around, inspecting everything, looking at every picture that was on the mantel.

"You seem nervous," I said as I took off my jacket, laying it across the arm of the couch.

Monica blushed lightly. She picked up a baby picture of me and my mother. Instead of Monica answering my question, she asked one of her own. "You looked
so innocent back then. What happened, Preacher?"

I slowly walked behind her, pretending to be looking at the picture, only to stand closely behind her so that she could feel what took away my innocence.

"First and foremost," I said, my lips close to her ears and my cool mint breath sending chills down her spine. I pulled her to me, her back rested against my chest. "Don't call me Preacher. Call me, X, or Xzavier. Secondly, what did you mean by that? Am I not innocent anymore?" My lips hovered over her ear as I breathed slowly on her neck. Her head fell to the side, giving me more access to her neck.

As I moved in to kiss her neck, she walked out of my embrace, denying me, like an incorrect password. I let my hands fall to my side as I watched her walk away. God, how I hated chasing after my food.

"Your innocence is proven only after you have proved that you aren't guilty, right?" she asked as she continued to walk around as if she was avoiding me.

I smiled. She was like a canned tuna. Wild catch. She roamed around my den as if she was in the water. No matter what she did, she would eventually get caught. And Lord knows, as soon as I caught her, she was going to get ate. Finger lickin' good. So, I played her little game. The chase me so I won't feel easy game. I was down to play with her. Since she knew the game so well, she had to know how to really play it. And if she really knew how to play the game, then she had to know that the dick always won in the end. I mean, that was the only rule.

"Prove my innocence?" I asked.

Monica looked at me and smiled. "Yes, are you having a hard time?"

"In fact, I guess I am. I seem to have a little problem. I don't know what I'm being charged with."

Monica stared into my eyes from a short distance. She licked her lips, coating them with her saliva. They looked juicy, and wet. "You are being charged with making me sin. For making my pussy wet with lust. For making me want to be baptized in your semen."

I know for an average Joe, one would be shocked to hear a woman of Monica caliber speak so truthfully. But I'm not an average Joe. I get that all the time. Women always speak to me in such precise, passionate ways. What would catch me off guard is if a woman was to tell me that she isn't into me, or that I don't turn her on. Now that would leave me shocked.

I looked at Monica. Even though the words came out of her mouth, I could still sense she wasn't ready. I walked around the table that she had used to gain distance between us like her bodyguard. I stood face to face with her, my body anxious to prove my innocence.

"You know, Monica. Sins start in the mind, right."

Monica looked into my eyes, wanting me to make the first move, but wanting to do it herself.

"I know, X but how do I stop it? I tell myself that I'm stronger. That I should just go home and pray. What do I do? How do I keep my innocence when I'm already guilty in my mind?"

"I'll tell you how," I said as I closed the gap between us. Our bodies heated the room. I moved my hand up to her cheek, slowly caressing it. Monica tilted her head, her eyes closed. "We do it, without thought."

I kissed her lips softly. She kissed me back. Her kiss was gentle, passionate. Our lips broke away slowly, as if they had hurt to do so. "Let me be the one to commit the sin. I'll be the demon. I'll be the one to take all the blame. So, when they cast the first stone, it'll be at me."

"And what about when they cast the second stone, X? What'll happen then?" she asked, looking deep into my eyes for an answer.

"Then, I'll jump in front of you and let the stone they cast strike me. Like I said once before, there is nothing wrong with wanting something that you shouldn't have!"

"But, if we actually go through with this, then you'll have me," she clarified.

"I'll have your flesh, but your soul is yours to keep."

She looked at me as her head hung. "What about my heart? What if I catch feelings for you, X?"

"Then I'll make sure to protect your heart until you're ready for it back."

Monica nodded. I wasn't sure if she really agreed with what I was saying, or if she nodded to try to convince herself. "Okay," she said then sighed.

"I tell you what. If it makes you feel better. So that it don't feel like a reality, take us to your fantasy." I held her face in my hands and kissed her lips softly. Her arms wrapped around my shoulders as she raised to her tiptoes. A moan escaped and traveled into my mouth.

"What do you want me to do?" she asked. She sounded as if she was ready to follow me across the world and battle anyone that got in our way.

My right hand gripped her ass. It felt super soft, like a pillow, but warm, like someone had been sleeping on it. "Sing. You said that your fantasy was to have people make love to your singing. Why not sing, while making love?"

"Sing one of my songs?" she asked.

"Whatever you prefer to sing," I said as I kissed all over her neck.

"Uhmm. I-I don't know what to sing."

"Uhm, just follow my lead," I said as I looked into her eyes and began to sing the first song that came to mind. "I know it ain't all that late, but you should probably leave. And I recognize that look in your eyes. Yeah, you should probably leave." I started the song off as Monica finished where I stopped.

"Cause I know you and you know me, and we both know where this is gonna lead. You want me to say that I want you to stay, so you should probably leave."

Monica sung as I began to unbutton her shirt. I looked at her as she continued to sing. Her eyes were closed, yet her lips never stopped moving.

Monica's shirt fell to the floor as I unhooked the last button. Her skin looked smooth. I could see her excitement poking through her black laced bra. I buried my face between her perfect set of twins as she never missed a line of Chris Stapleton's hit song, You Should Probably Leave. As I kissed between her twins, I could smell the exact spot where she had sprayed her perfume.

I kissed the spot, leaving my own scent, my own mark. I took a step back. Her eyes were closed, but if I knew the lyrics to the song correctly, she was nearing the end of the song. My hand reached under her skirt. My fingers brushed against her covered sex. Monica flinched from my touch, her voice shuddered, making her perfect singing sound like a scratched-up CD.

"Sun on your skin, six a.m., And I been watching you sleep." Monica continued to sing. I might've been mistaken, but I could've sworn she already sung that part.

I started at Monica as she kept her eyes closed tight, remaining in her fantasy, afraid of her true reality. Her and I, me and her, sinning, and the only audience was the man upstairs himself. I reached behind Monica, searching for her zipper like a lost set of keys. Hitting jackpot, I eased her zipper down, her skirt fell down to her feet. I knew Monica felt it, but she still kept her eyes closed tight.

"Sun on your skin, six a.m., And I been watching you sleep." Monica sung.

I knew I wasn't crazy. That made three times she sung the same part. If I had to guess, it was to keep her in her fantasy. Because once the song stopped, so did her fantasy.

I grabbed Monica's hand, slowly, gently pulling her to me. She stepped out of her skirt, standing directly in front of me. She crossed her legs shyly.

If she was still singing, I wouldn't be able to tell you, I was too focused on the gap between her legs. Monica had what you would call a box. Perfectly shaped, evenly cut into perfection. I shook my head as I stared at her covered sex. Her panties held her meaty box like a fat kid holds the last piece of cake. Monica stood before me looking as if she was actually modeling her panty and bra set. She looked that beautiful. I quietly walked behind Monica to get a closer look at her backside. And if I could get a witness in here tonight, I know everyone would agree that her backside was just as beautiful as the front.

My body shivered from just the excitement I knew I was bringing to her body. I loved women, and all of their glory. The one thing a man couldn't live without. Women were amazing. There was nothing like a woman looking thick in her sweats. Or the way her ass would bounce in a sundress. Or the way their lingerie cut perfectly with their every curve. Lord knows nothing could compare to it. But the one thing I loved, was when a woman could look beautiful with clothes on, but like a goddess when she was naked.

I reached out, determined to show Monica she was a true goddess. I unhooked the safety on her bra, setting off two shots deep in my balls. I couldn't wait to get my hands on them, so I walked up to her, my dick pressing against her soft ass. I reached around her. I fumbled her right titty; her nipple was already hard as a rock. I pulled it lightly, but I squeezed the tip as her head fell back on my shoulder. Monica's hand reached behind her in between us as she reached for my dick. As she gripped my dick, she went for my zipper, determined to feel the real thing.

As Monica pulled my zipper down, she anxiously reached inside my pants and gripped my dick. I was without boxers, so she had easy access. She pulled my dick out and rubbed it against her soft ass cheeks smearing precum all over them. I reached around her and placed my thumb inside her thin material that she called panties. I eased them down just under her mound. I squatted behind her, inspecting her hole, looking for the perfect spot to land my wet tongue.

I gripped both of her ass cheeks in my hands. I was a little rough, but my tongue was gentle as I swiped her juicy sex lips back and forth.

"Uhm, God!" Monica moaned as I gripped her ass tighter and stuck my tongue deep inside of her box. I fucked her tight hole with my tongue, my nose invaded her crinkled hole every time my tongue went in and out. Her body smelt amazing. I could've buried my nose in the crack of her ass and left it there for good.

Monica slowly eased to the couch, determined to escape my superb tongue game. I crawled after her, my pants still on, but my dick was out like a free man on parole. It was only so much it could do with all the restrictions. Monica raised her right leg and placed her foot flat on the arm of the couch. She bent at the waist; I looked up at her beautiful box with my mouth wide open. Monica looked over her shoulders at me, no words left her mouth, but I could definitely read her mind.

Monica's left hand reached under her in between her legs. She rubbed her wet pussy smearing her juices all over her thick lips. She brought her fingers to her mouth and spat saliva on them. She reached back under her and massaged her clit as she moaned to herself. The sight was so beautiful all I could do was watch. My dick was hard, so hard that I thought it would burst. As Monica continued to play with her clit, I stood to my feet. I unbuttoned my pants and let them fall to too floor. My shirt came off so fast I know if there was a record for it, I just broke it. I slowly walked up behind Monica as she was caught up in her own playground. I knelt behind her, using her ass cheeks for balance. I spread her soft cheeks and stuck my tongue in and out of her asshole at a rapid speed.

"Ohhh, you so nasty!" Monica moaned as she played with her clit. I nodded in agreement. I was a nasty motherfucker. I wasn't going to deny it. I wasn't like some men that feel disgusted when a woman pass gas. Nah, I was a man's man. I didn't feel some type of way when a woman takes a shit with the door open. I loved everything about a woman. And I do mean, everything.

I tongued fucked Monica's ass so good that she damned near fell over the arm of the couch. Monica's juices creamed down her thighs as she came back-to-back. As Monica's body spasmed from her orgasm, I slapped her on the ass as I stood to my feet. Monica was no longer the same. She was no longer singing for her fantasy. She no longer needed the motivation. She was fully motivated, and fully aroused. Monica turned to face me. She was now the guilty one. And if I was the reason for her losing her innocence, then I plead the fifth.

My dick stood out, hard and anxious in front of me. Long twin veins ran across each other, blood pumping through them. My sexual adrenaline was at an all-time high. Monica looked at me as her chest panted up and down. Her breathing was heavy, slow and deep. She stared into my eyes, hypnotized by what my tongue did to her insides. Monica walked up to me slowly, the entire time she stared into my eyes. As she stood face to face with me, she grabbed my dick as squeezed it in her tight hand.

Monica's legs spread, she reached between her legs to her slippery box. She stuck two fingers in her hole and brought them back out. Her fingers soaked with her juices, Monica gripped my dick with her slippery hand and stroked my hard dick as she stared into my eyes.

"X', I've never came so hard in all of my life. What did you just do to me? Monica asked as she continued to stroke my dick up and down while looking directly in my eyes.

"Uhh.." I groaned as she gripped my dick. "I did exactly what you wanted me to do?"

Monica stopped abruptly as she looked at me. "What are you talking about?" she asked.

I looked at her like she was crazy as she held my dick in her hand. "You wanted to be free from the bondage you've been in your whole life. To experience a lust so real that from this day forward love will always be fake. I only gave you the reality of your fantasy."

Monica's mouth fell open as she stared at me. The grip she had on my dick loosened as she fell down to her knees in front of me. Monica licked her tongue out swiping the head of my dick with it. She reached out and grabbed it, smacking her tongue with the head.

I looked down her throat, her tonsils were my target. Monica sucked me into her warm mouth. Her dimples showed in her cheeks as she worked her jaws around me. I closed my eyes and rocked my hips as the feeling took over.

Monica looked into my eyes as soon as I opened them. I couldn't help but think about how wet her mouth was. I could only hope that her insides were just as wet and warm.

"Monica, please!" I begged as she deep throated me. Monica made a slurping sound, then her mouth made a popping sound as my dick came out of her mouth. Spit dripped from her mouth to the floor. She didn't even wipe her mouth as she smiled at me. She called me nasty though.

"What, did I do something wrong?" she asked as she slowly stroked her spit around my dick.

"Stand yo' sexy ass up." I demanded.

Monica's smile faded. The look she had wasn't lust, but obsession. I gave her a helping hand as she stood to her feet. Having her stand in front of me completely naked, unclothed with her nakedness on full display, it was a beautiful sight. I wondered if Adam felt the same for Eve the first time he really realized she was naked. Did he get an erection as hard as the one I had right now. Damn, why did Eve have to eat that apple, making us realize how beautiful our bodies really were. And yet everyone blamed the devil for them eating the apple. Eve knew how beautiful she was. I can imagine she probably walked past a stream and saw her reflection in the water. Her curves, her flat stomach, the nappy hairs covering her sex. She knew God had invented a secret weapon. A weapon that made mankind bow down to their knees. The same way I was bowing down to Monica only minutes before with my tongue between her glory. Rotten apple!

I held Monica's hand in mine as I turned my back to her taking the lead. I knew she was maybe thinking we were about to go to my room and finish what the devil started. Nah, I had something else on my mind . As we made it to my back sliding door that led to my backyard, I slid the curtain back so we both could have a clear view of my backyard. I pulled Monica's hand lightly bringing her in front of me. She walked up to the glass and looked out the glass door. I walked up behind her, sandwiching her between the glass. I kissed all over her neck. She gave me access to her sweet spots. I guess I finally got the passwords correct.

My hand snaked under her legs and found her clit. I massaged it, circling it at a steady pace. Monica spread her legs. I could feel the heat coming from her body. The lust, the want, the need. She reached behind me and found my dick. She felt safe with me, no bodyguard, no gun, no mace. She didn't care about protection; she just slowly slid me inside of her tight pussy.

The moonlight lit up the night sky. The stars were out, but that wasn't what made the night so amazing. Monica moaned as I stroked her pussy to perfection. She raised her arms above her head and placed them on the glass. Her legs spread more, giving me more room to work my magic.

"X, lord knows you are an amazing lover," she cooed as I stroked her.

I had both of her cheeks spread with my hands as I watched my dick move in and out of her hole. "Monica baby, do you see what I see?" I asked with my lips close to her ear.

"Mmmm, see what?" she asked.

"Open your eyes and look outside. Tell me what you see?" I asked her as I continued to deep stroke her.

Monica looked outside into the night and looked around. "Oh my God, that feels so... good," she moaned.

"Tell daddy what you see," I said not missing a stroke.

"Ohh daddy, I see… a fuck!" She moaned.

I kissed all over her neck trailing them to her ear. I kissed all over her ear then I lightly bit it, pulling it with my teeth.

"Tell me," I said softly in her ear. "What do you see?"

"I see, a patio set," she said as she humped backwards into my midsection.

"What else?" I asked as I plunged my entire dick in the bottom of her pussy and stayed there.

"Ahhhh, fuck!" she screamed as she fogged up the glass door.

"Tell daddy what else do you see?"

"Ohh, daddy .... I see a tree," she said as I rocked my hips in a circular motion.

I smiled behind her sexy ass as I felt her cum on my dick. "You see that tree, babe. You asked me earlier what took my innocence. It was that tree. See, that tree is an apple tree. That same tree is what took your innocence. The tree of good and evil. We are born to be both good, and evil. That's what I learned my whole life in church. That's the point of having free will. To decide if you want to be good, or evil. Each day you have a choice. You just have to choose wisely," I said as I pulled out and came all over her ass cheeks.

My dick spasmed in spurts as my hot cum splattered all over her ass. Monica stayed still as she let me paint her ass with my cream. The entire time I came, she was looking out the window at my apple tree. As the last of my semen dripped out of the head onto her ass, I took a step back and looked at her look at the tree. I knew at that moment she was thinking the same thing I thought earlier. Rotten apple!

Xtasy

Chapter 7
Xzavier

Beep! Beep! Beep! Beep! Beep! My alarm went off letting me know that it was already 6:00am. I reached over without raising my head to snooze the alarm. I yawned as I rolled over on my back. I was still exhausted from me and Monica's session the night before. We had sex so much last night that my balls are sore from her bouncing up and down on them all night. I literally had to put her out to get some sleep. I mean, not *literally literally*, but yeah. Before Monica left for the night, we exchanged numbers. Would I call her? Of course. Monica was a dime plus a nickel. And let's not forget she had some amazing pussy. Her head wasn't the best, but it wasn't the worst that I've ever had. But I did fuck up really bad. Monica ended up telling me that she was committing herself to my father's church. She was actually going to start singing in the choir right alongside Ria with Rudy as their choir director.

At dinner, I only wanted to molest her mind so she would give her body to me freely. And my plan worked. But it backfired. I fucked Monica so good that she would've changed her religion if I had asked her to. I knew it would end up being weird with her always around me. And that's the only negative thing that comes with having some good dick.

As I sat up in the bed, I couldn't help but stretch. My entire body felt sore, like I had been in the gym working out. I tossed the covers to the side and stood up. I clapped my hands twice for the lights to come on. I wasn't the lazy type, I just always found clap-on lights to be very interesting,

I stretched the band on my boxer briefs to let some air in my boxers as I walked to the bathroom. I walked to the toilet to release my morning wood. I looked at the picture that I had mounted above the toilet. It was a picture of four dogs playing poker. I laughed as I shook the last bit of pee out. The picture never got old to me. It actually made my mornings every morning.

After I flushed the toilet, I walked to the sink and washed my hands. I grabbed my toothbrush from the charger then squeezed some Sensodyne toothpaste onto it. I turned the toothbrush on and began to brush my teeth. As I rinsed my mouth out, I heard my cell chime with a text message notification. I wiped my face as I walked in the bedroom. I picked my phone up and saw that I had a text message from Monica. She was thanking me for the awesome night last night. She even hinted at doing it again soon. She only got the one-night stand deal last night. She didn't get the deluxe package. I texted her back with a happy face emoji then I sat my phone down.

I kneeled beside my bed and placed my hands together to pray. It was a force of habit of me to pray after I brush my teeth. I know it all might sound weird. A sex addict, praying. Every morning. I mean, I am in fact a sex addict. I'm not ashamed to say I'm addicted to sex. Unless, you're my mother or father or anyone close to them. But me being addicted to sex does not make me the devil. I just have devilish ways, that's all.

After I finished thanking the lord for the amazing night I had last night, and for waking me up to see another day, I stood to my feet and stretched again. For some reason I felt exhausted. It was a good thing that my day job was working at the church. I would be able to sneak in a few extra hours of sleep once I got in my office.

"Hello, brother Xzavier. How are you this morning?" Sister Joanne asked as I parked my Porsche truck in my very own parking spot. I gave Sister Joanne a smile as I rolled the windows up. I killed the engine then I stepped out the truck looking like a collection plate for T.D. Jakes church.

I always kept my attire up to par. I represented my father, so I always made sure I stepped out with my clothes starched down, with nothing but the latest fashion. I was very debonair. I vowed to never let a soul, especially a woman, see me off my square. I wanted my every impression to be the best impression. My closet was laced with Gucci, Prada, Ralph Lauren, Tom Ford, Louis Vuitton, and Armani. I also had two closets full of designer shoes. I'm very particular about my appearance.

"Good morning, Sister Joanne. You're here early this morning." I gave her a sideways hug.

Sister Joanne was my mother's personal secretary. They had been friends for as long as I could remember. I reached out and grabbed the box that Sister Joanne was carrying.

"Thank you," she said then smiled. "Your father cut up yesterday, didn't he?"

I nodded then said, "Don't he always." I laughed.

Sister Joanne nodded then said, "Yes, he does. You know Xzavier, I can wait for him to retire, but I'm also excited to see how great you'll be when he does."

As we walked to the front of the church, I stayed silent. I couldn't understand why everyone automatically placed me behind my father's pulpit. It annoyed the hell out of me. I didn't let it show though. I was good at hiding shit.

I opened the front door to the church and held it with my back as Sister Joanne walked inside. I wanted to finally tell Sister Joanne what I've been dying to tell everyone else for the longest, but I for one didn't know how to put the words together. I really wasn't ready to expose the big secret that everyone didn't know about. So, I just stayed silent like I always did.

As we made it to Sister Joanne's office, I sat the box down on her desk then turned to walk away.

"Brother Xzavier, is something wrong?" Sister Joanne asked.

I sighed as I turned to face her. I looked directly in her eyes wondering what she would say if I was to really tell her what I was thinking. I knew she wouldn't, so I just said, "Nothing Sister Joanne. I'm great," I said it with a straight face. Sister Joanne smiled as she walked closer to me.

Sister Joanne placed her hand on my shoulder and said, "You know I've been knowing you since you were in diapers. Me and your mother have been friends for as long as I could remember. Before you were born actually. You're family, so if you ever need someone to talk to, I'm always here."

I nodded as I held my tears in. It hurt me to not be able to tell anyone that I wanted nothing to do with my father's pulpit, and his church. I wanted my own life. To be able to walk in my own shoes, and not have to fill his. But I really had no one I could actually talk to about it who really wouldn't judge me. Sure, Sister Joanne was telling me that I could talk to her about anything. But if I was to tell her what I was feeling, I would end up sending her to an early grave with the news.

"Thank you, Sister Joanne. I'll keep that in mind," I said as we hugged.

I walked out of her office, closing the door behind me. I placed my back against the side wall and took a deep breath. I didn't know how long I would be able to hold my secret in, especially since everyone has been talking as if my father was about to really retire soon.

I let my head hang. I listened closely as I heard a gospel song coming from the indoor gym. I stood up straight as I listened to the music wondering who was playing it. I strolled in the direction of the music. It was a Monday morning. Choir rehearsal wasn't until Tuesday, so it confused me to hear gospel music coming from the gym.

As I made it to the gym doors, I stuck my head inside and took a look around. There was a woman standing off in the distance with her back to me. She wore a pair of black cotton leggings with a scarf wrapped around her waist. Her black sleeveless shirt matched her scarf. I continued to watch her as she slowly began to dance to the music. Her dance wasn't something you would see on a day-to-day basis. Her hips moved in symbolic motion. Like she had learned to dance in a tribe in Kenya. Her motions began to tell a story as she moved to the words of the song. I knew she was doing a praise dance, but deep down inside, I was praying that she would start twerking to the beat.

As the song ended, the woman pressed pause on her stereo. She bent over and grabbed a towel to wipe her face. I looked at her ass as she cleaned her face. Once she finished wiping her face, she tossed the towel to the side and then pressed play on her stereo. She turned in my direction as she began to restart her dance routine. She looked at me and smiled as the song started over. As the song began, Sonja ran over to the stereo and pressed pause. She faced me and asked, "How long have you been standing there?"

"Not long as I should've been," I said under my breath. Sonja looked at me confused and said, "What did you say?"

I shook my head as I held in a laugh. "Nothing. I didn't say anything. Uhh, how's everything going so far? Have you thought of how you'll have everything lined up?"

"Yes, I have. I thought about talking to a lot of young women in the Bible study classes to see if they wanted to join."

I nodded and said, "That's a great idea."

"I also thought about making some signs and placing them on the bulletin board so people could see."

"Have you thought of what everyone would wear?"

"Not really. That's a great question." Sonja looked up at the ceiling as if she was thinking of a master plan.

She walked off in the direction her towel and bent over to grab a bottle of water. I matched her as she bent over at the waist without bending her knees. Her pussy print peeked from under her scarf. I couldn't help but wonder how sweaty her pussy was. I figured she probably sprayed perfume all over her pussy before she got dressed. With all the dancing she's been doing, I can guarantee her perfume sweated off by now. I'd bet my religion that she still smelled amazing.

Sonja stood straight up with her back to me. She moved her weight to her back leg making her ass poke out. My dick grew inside my slacks as I watched her. Sonja was a sight to see. Ever since the moment I laid eyes on her in church, I've had this crush of lust on her that I couldn't explain, or contain.

"Hey, Sonja. I mean, Ms. Echols. I should go. I have a lot of paperwork to do. Uhm, but if you need anything, my office is down the hall."

Sonja nodded as she placed the cap on her water. "Of course. I should also get back to creating material just in case I find someone who'd want to learn and perform with me."

I nodded as. I placed my hand in front of my hard-on. I had to get to my office, and quick, or I would have to get a new pair of pants.

"I'll be seeing you around," I said as I walked away. I looked over my shoulder. I could've sworn I saw Sonja looking at my ass as I walked out the gym. I laughed to myself. I thought that that was only something men did.

Chapter 8
Donnie

"Henry, I need a big favor," I said as I stood at the bar of one of my favorite hole-in-the wall gambling shacks, Outta Luck.

Donnie, I'm all out of favors for you. I almost got my head put on a chopping block for loaning you money when you hadn't paid us back from the last time from the previous loan. Fish ain't going to have more head all because of you. I'm sorry," Henry, the bartender explained.

Henry was the best bartender at Outta Luck. Henry and I went way back. We actually only lived a couple of houses down from each other. It was Henry who introduced me to Outta Luck. One day we were just hanging out, and he asked me if I wanted to grab a few drinks with him. I accepted and we ended up going to Outta Luck.

Outta Luck is mainly a small bar in the front, and a gambling shack in the very back. That day, as me and Henry were knocking back a few shots, Henry leans over and whispers to me that behind the bar is a fake wall hiding a casino. He informed me that if a certain nozzle was pulled down in a specific combination, the entire bar would turn in a three-hundred-and-sixty-degree axis and we'll be in another room with half naked women, poker tables, slot machines, and crap tables.

Now, I was drunk, but I wasn't no fool. I knew Henry was just pulling my leg, and I told him just that. Henry made me an offer or a bet so to say. He bet me that if I could show him five hundred dollars in cash, and also pay the entry fee of another hundred bucks, he would show me the so-called casino. I ordered us another shot, and bet Henry that I would pay him every dime I had in my pocket that he was a plum liar. I pulled my money out my pocket, which was fifteen hundred in cash safety secured between my gold-plated money clip that my wife Sonja bought me for my birthday and slapped it on the bar top.

Henry gets up with this big cheesy grin on his face as he walks towards the beer nozzles on his left side and waves me over beside him. Henry grabs an empty beer jug then he pulls down the

Heineken beer nozzle along with a red nozzle. All of a sudden it starts to feel as if the ground is moving underneath us. As the bar is moving, the people sitting inside the bar isn't. I closed my eyes thinking that I had one too many to drink. As the ground stopped moving, I opened my eyes to a bright light. In fact, the whole room was lit up with lights. I looked to the side at Henry. He wore the same cheesy smile, only this time he had his hand held flat out to me. I looked around the room. There were men and women gambling all around us. There were poker tables, slot machines, crap tables, even half naked women exactly how Henry had described it. I handed henry every dollar that I had on me. I slapped it in his hand without looking his way.

Henry stepped off the bar leading the way. "Welcome, to Outta Luck!" Henry said smiling.

I looked around in awe. For years I had heard of underground gambling shacks hiding in plain sight in Houston. But never did I expect to be inside of one. Henry nudged me with his elbow. I looked down at his hand. "Here, you'll need something to try your luck with. But, if you lose it all, you're outta luck."

I laughed as I accepted half of my money back. "What was that the motto or something?" I asked as I followed behind Henry.

"I guess you can say that," Henry said as he led us to an empty blackjack table. "You play?" he asked.

"Only online. Never played it in a real casino before." I sat down at the empty seat beside Henry. The dealer was a female, a beautiful Asian woman with short dark brown hair. She wore a black strapless dress that showed off her cleavage. I looked around the room at all the other men and women winning and losing their money. Some wore a smile, and others look defeated.

I watched as Henry slid five hundred of my money across the table to the dealer.

Henry looked at me as I counted out three hundred dollars and slid it across the table.

"That's all you're going to play with, three hundred dollars?" Henry asked as he played with his chips with his hands.

As I received my chips, I stacked them up in colors. "Yeah, I already got beat out of half of my money by you. If I lose this, I'm done."

"If you say so."

The dealer grabbed two fresh decks of cards and began to shuffle them. She did some fancy trick with the cards, then she placed them in a card holder. She looked up at me with a beautiful smile. "Players, place your bets."

I looked to Henry as he placed a fifty-dollar chip in his circle. I grabbed a twenty-dollar chip and placed it on mines. As the dealer reached for the first card, Henry raised his hand to her. She waited as he placed another fifty-dollar chip on the left side of him at an empty seat. Henry looked to me and smiled. Losing my money wasn't going to hurt him, and he was showing me just that.

"Last bets," the dealer said looking from me to Henry. She nodded then pulled a card from the top of the deck and placed it in front of me. She grabbed another card from the top of the deck and placed it in front of Henry, then she did the same to the empty seat beside Henry. She grabbed another card from the top of the deck and placed it in front of herself.

I looked around at all the cards. The dealer had a king of diamond. Henry had a queen of spades, and I had a measly three of clubs. The dealer placed another card in front of me facing down, then Henry, and the same to the empty seat beside Henry. Then, she placed one beside her king.

"Hit me," I said, hoping for something good to come off the top of the deck.

As the dealer pulled the top card from the deck, she flipped it up and placed it beside my measly three of clubs. I smiled. I had just received a jack of diamonds, which was good, so far. The dealer looked at me. "Hit me," I said hoping for something small.

As she flipped the card from the top of the deck and placed it beside my other cards, I smiled. I had just received a four of hearts.

"Stay," I said smiling.

The dealer looked to Henry. He shook his hand indicating that he wanted to stay. The dealer stayed as well. I flipped my hidden card over and hung my head low as my smile faded. I stared in the face of a king of clubs. I had just lost my first twenty dollars gambling at Outta Luck. I looked to the side as Henry flipped over an ace of spade. He had won. With my money. The dealer flipped over her card and showed an eight of clubs. I shook my head.

That day was the start of my downfall. It was that day that I became addicted to gambling. That day I had lost all of money, and then I borrowed some. That was the day my addiction started and the day I got myself into debt, and it stayed that way. It's been almost a year since I was introduced to Outta Luck, and to this day, my luck still hasn't changed.

Chapter 9
The Next Day
Xzavier

I walked inside The Lord's Manna with a smile on my face. It was days like this that I really enjoyed coming to church. Today, Rudy invited me in to listen to one of his choir rehearsals, not like I really needed an invitation. But today would be the first rehearsal with Ria and Monica singing in the choir. I had already heard a few songs with the two of them singing together, and I had already got a solo session from Monica the other night, which was a night to remember.

After me and Monica's night together, I had yet to call her. After she sent me that text, I sent her a short one back, mainly a smiley face. But I knew she got my point. I wasn't really the relationship kind of guy, and I didn't want her to get the wrong idea, so I haven' t called.

I walked inside the main section of the church as Rudy and the entire choir was setting up to rehearse. Rudy was standing at the front of the stage placing all the new singers in their proper sections. I looked up at Ria as I walked up to the stage. She wore this big smile on her face as she noticed me. Ria was a beautiful woman. She wasn't as bad as Monica, but she did have a helluva shape on her. Ria was on the thick side. Not fat, but juicy. She had hips and a lot of ass that made her look short and thick. She was close to five foot five, with fairly large, but perfect tits. Her hair was short, cut into a Halle Berry style. Ria's skin was smooth, light skinned, with some nice juicy lips. Today, she wore some red lipstick. She came to rehearsal with a classy, but comfy look. She wore a pair of grey loose Nike joggers with a grey V-neck to match.

I looked to the side of Ria to Monica. Now Monica was a sight to see. Monica was brown skinned with a long ponytail. The last time I saw her she was completely naked in my house, in my bed, with her hair in one ponytail with a single braid down the right side. Today, she had her hair in a long ponytail, but she had dyed it with strawberry streaks. She also wore a set of joggers just like Ria.

Monica wasn't as thick as Ria, so she didn't fill her joggers out as much, but she did have a beautiful body naked. Monica could've been a runway model if she wanted to. She had the looks, the smile, and the figure.

Monica looked at me as she noticed me and smiled.

Rudy had to have noticed the both of them smiling as he turned around to see what was taking all of his shine. "My main man. You're here early today," Rudy said, playing it off like he didn't invite me.

I took the steps to the stage and hugged him. "Yeah, I had a lot of paperwork to do today, so I figured I'll come in early to take care of it. How's everything going with these two beautiful ladies?" I asked Rudy as I looked from Monica to Ria. They both smiled at my comment.

"You're actually right on time, we haven't even started yet. We were just getting set up. You should listen in and tell me what you think."

I waved my hand. "Nah, I don't want to intrude. Plus, I have so much paperwork to do. I can't," I said.

Ria stepped up to us. "Come on, Xzavier, we don't mind if you sit in and listen. We're going to be your choir soon anyhow."

I smiled, but on the inside, I wasn't amused. I hated when people just tried to place me at the altar.

"I can't," I said.

"Come on X, it'll mean a lot to us," Monica said. It was the first time I actually heard her voice since the night she screamed for me to go deeper.

I looked at my watch. "I guess I can spare a few minutes," I said causing them all to smile. Monica stepped up to me. I pulled her in for a hug. I could feel her breath on my neck as we hugged. All eyes were on us as we embraced. I could feel the rooms stares. It wasn't nothing special, it was only a hug. But I knew people were going to paint it as so much more. If only they knew what we did the other night. That would really give them something to talk about.

I hugged Ria afterwards, just to throw everyone off. As me and Ria hugged, I could feel her titties pressed hard against my chest.

As our hug broke off, I walked up to the drummer, Pop. Pop had been with the church around the same time as Rudy had been. Pop's real name is Darius. Pop was younger than Rudy and I by a few years. Pop and I became close friends through Rudy. Rudy and Pop came up singing together in a small gospel competition. Pop was a damn good drummer. The best I've heard so far.

Pop was around five foot nine. At one point in time, he weighed almost three hundred pounds, He came to me with the problem of him wanting to lose weight, so I asked him to be my workout partner. Pop lost weight like it didn't belong there. He was a natural. I told him once before that if he wasn't a drummer, he could've been the face for Weight Watchers.

"Pop, tell me something good," I said as we shook hands. Pop fixed his Tom Ford glasses on his face and sat down behind the drums. He rubbed his hand across his waves and said, "Enjoying this beautiful Tuesday morning and don't forget this beautiful view," Pop said, nudging towards Monica and Ria.

I laughed and said, "Alright Pop, let your wife find out you're getting your glasses all fogged up looking at other women, she'll starve you to death."

Pop laughed, then he grabbed his drum sticks and hit the drums as if I had just made a joke. "Baby ain't gon' ever starve me, I'm the breadwinner. I bring home the bacon."

"So, what do you think about 'em?" I asked of Ria and Monica as I turned my back to the drums looking in their direction.
"If I had my choice, I'll take the thick one. But you know that's my preference. The one on the left is way prettier though," Pop said, speaking of Monica.

I smiled. Monica was a dime. "You know me, and Rudy went out with them the other night. It wasn't nothing special, just conversation. Monica got a nice head on her shoulders."

Pop shoved me and laughed. "If she does, you' re the man to know, huh."

I smiled as I looked at Monica. She somehow felt me looking at her. She turned and looked at me with that beautiful smile.

"Who. Is. That?" Pop asked.

I followed his eyes in the direction of the front door. "That's! That's Sonja, I mean Ms. Echols. She's the new praise dance team instructor," I said as I watched Sonja walk up to the stage looking like a fresh Hershey bar.

I loved all kinds of women. I didn't discriminate. I liked big, juicy women. Short and thick. Tall and skinny. Hell, I didn't get too picky when it came to women. But there is something special about a beautiful, dark-skinned woman with some smooth skin, and an amazing smile. Now that, that combination, I guess you can say, is my top pick. And Sonja was all that plus more.

"She's... beautiful," Pop said from behind me. I didn't reply to his comment. I was too busy trying to get myself out of the trance Sonja had me in.

I walked in Sonja's direction.

"X', we 're about to start," Rudy said as I was walking down the stairs. I only nodded as I walked past him.

I stopped directly in front of Sonja. I thought for sure Monica had the most beautiful smile, but Sonja took the cake.

"I figured you'll be in here," Sonja said joking directly in my eyes. I found it extremely sexy when a woman looked me directly in the eyes. Sonja's stare was dangerous, and contagious. She looked deep into my eyes without breaking eye contact.

"You were looking for me, for?" I asked, trying not to sound too excited to see her.

"I was told that if I needed any help that I should come see you, per your father," she said then smiled.

"I was in the middle of something, but what can I assist you with?" I looked at her, wondering what she needed my help with. Not like it mattered. She could've asked me for anything. I would've done it. And I do mean, anything.

"I just finished coming up with this new dance. I was wondering if you could come and look in on me as I went over it again. That's if you're up to it. I know you're a very busy man, so if you can't I understand."

I thought about what Drake said in one of his songs. I might come, I might go. I don't know. Nah, who was I kidding, I was damn sure going. "I guess I can assist you."

Sonja smiled and took the lead to her domain. Just as I began to walk behind her, the choir began to sing. I hung my head and held my finger up to excuse myself.

"Just take a seat," Sonja said as we made it inside the gym where she had been rehearsing. She had yet to accomplish getting anyone to join her dance team, so it was just me and her. I took the only available seat in the center of the floor. On the back of the chair was a black Reebok jacket. I watched as Sonja walked over to her stereo system. She bent over without bending her knees and pressed play.

Sonja wore a pair of red and pink leggings. As she bent over, I could see her fat pussy print from the back, but no panty line. If I had to guess, she was probably wearing a thong. Now, let me clear the air, I'm far from jealous man, but I do envy women's clothing. especially the thong. Thongs were able to give women the sixty-nine without any conversation. Some people say that when we die, we come back as someone else. Being honest, if it was true, I wouldn't want to come back as any human. I would want to come back as a woman's thong, just saying.

Sonja's choice of song started. She had her back turned to me, her arms frozen in place above her head.

Party girls don't get hurt. Can't feel anything, when will I learn I push it down, push it down. I'm the one for a good time call. Phone's blowin' up, ringing my doorbell. I feel the love, feel the love. One, two, three, one, two three, drink.

My mouth fell open in complete shock as Sonja danced to the beat. Her body moved in a different sync. She wasn't doing a praise dance. She was dancing as if the Gods were praising her. My mouth hung open. I leaned back in my seat and opened my legs wide. My dick jumped in my pants. My blood was pumping, waking up the master of the house. My dick controlled my life. It controlled my destiny, and my judgement day.

Throw 'em back 'til I lose count I'm gonna swing from the chandelier from the chandelier.
Sonja didn't pop her ass. She didn't twerk but the way she danced, she could've easily put Ciara to shame. Her moves were exotic, and erotic. As she danced, I stood to my feet. Her moves had my legs hypnotized. Like I wasn't controlling them. It was like her moves were controlling mine. I walked closer to her. I watched from a close distance, high definition. My arms moved out in front of me. I reached for her, but she danced away from my reach. I moved closer, aiming to join in with her. A dance of our own. Sonja walked backwards into me. She jumped and faced me in shock. Before she could utter a word, I grabbed her hand and pulled her into me. I placed my left hand on her hip and guided her steps in sync with mine.

Sonja looked up at me. Her eyes were piercing mine. I held her stare, unafraid of the depths her eyes were taking me to. They were full, wide as the ocean. But I was prepared. If I was to drown in them, I would die a happy man.

'Won't look down, won't open my eyes. Keep my glass full until the morning light. Cause I'm just holding on for tonight...
Our feet moved in sync to the beat. We were tangoing in a tangled web. We were trapped in a beat that only our hearts understood for the moment. I didn't know the words to the song that we were dancing to, but I hoped she had it on repeat. Sonja's eyes closed as I twirled her around. Her backside was to me. Her backside hugged my midsection like it had once known it but hadn't seen it in years. Our bodies swayed together as if they were one.

My dick was hard, so I knew without a doubt she felt him poking. Our legs stopped moving, I held her in my embrace. Neither of us saying anything. Neither of us moving. I leaned forward, lips moving to her ear. There was so much I wanted to say, but only with body language. Just as I went to kiss her neck, the CD started skipping.

The CD skipping brought Sonja back to reality as she escaped from my embrace. She ran over to the CD player and turned the music off. She faced me slowly, ashamed of what we had just done.

She looked down at my dick print. Her head hung from the sight. My dick print was a dead give a way. We were sinning in the house of the lord.

"I'm sorry," I said apologizing.

"No, it should be me apologizing. I was the one that asked you to come in and watch. And then the dance, the song, it wasn't appropriate. I didn't mean to get you like that," Sonja said, looking down at my print again.

"Sonja, if I can be honest, you could've danced to the Barney song, I still would feel the same way. It's you, not the song, or the dance."

Sonja smiled. Then it faded just as fast. "I should go." She grabbed her jacket from the back of the chair. I grabbed her arm. She froze from my touch. I was supposed to say something. I just know it. But no words came out. Hesitantly, I let her arm go. She never looked back at me as she walked out of the gym. Something told me to go after her, but I didn't. And I hoped one day I didn't regret it.

Xtasy

Chapter 10
Sonja

As I walked out of the gym, leaving Xzavier behind, my pussy ached for me to go back and let him get exactly what his dick desired. But I didn't go back. I had to run. If I stayed, I would've tarnished my marriage. And for what, some dick. Well, maybe not just any dick, because I could tell Xzavier had some good dick. And I do mean gooooood dick. When we were dancing, I could feel his dick pressed against my ass. It was hard, yet nicely snuggled against my soft cheeks. My eyes had closed unvoluntary. So bad that I wanted to let him take me in that position. To pull me close to his body and hold me there as I wiggled on his dick. But I didn't. We didn't. Not because I was married but because it wasn't the right time. And there was a time for everything.

I got behind the wheel of my four-door drop top Volkswagen. I sat inside and closed the door, then locked them. There was tint on the windows, so I wasn't worried about getting caught by wandering eyes. I tossed my jacket on the passenger seat and slid my seat back. I eased my ass off the seat then I pulled my leggings down under my ass, then my thong.

When I was feeling hot and bothered, I would usually look up porn on my phone, but this time it wouldn't be needed. All I wanted and needed to have on my mind this time was Xzavier's handsome face.

I spread my legs and lifted the right one across the middle console. My sex lips were already coated, glossy from my thought alone. I touched them, a shock went through my fingertips. It was like my sex lips were already sore from just imagining what Xzavier could do to them. I slowly massaged them, spreading my juices all over them. They looked as if I applied lip gloss to them. They felt swollen, plump, like ripe fruit. My eyes closed. I imagined Xzavier was in the passenger seat, watching me, staring, fascinated. I spread my legs wider. I wanted him to get a good view of my mountain peak.

My button peaked from behind the curtain into plain sight. It was swollen and tender. Wet and slippery from my juices. I placed my pointer finger on my clit and massaged it slowly as my eyes closed tight. My mouth opened as a moan escaped. I imagined my fingers were Xzavier's. I stuck my middle finger in my tight box, cum soaked my finger like a sponge. I stroked my insides with my finger at a slow, but steady pace. I imagined Xzavier's hands were mines. My touch was his. The heat from his body, I felt it. His deep baritone voice whispering in my ear, telling me how wet and tight my pussy was. I began to strum my pearl as if it were strings from an acoustic guitar. I switched hands. Moving my right hand across the console as if I was reaching for his dick, I envisioned how big it was.

When we were dancing, I felt the size, the strength, mushing my ass. It felt strong, powerful, like the word of God. I imagined that I unzipped his pants, then stuck my hand in them and freed his massive cucumber dick. I played with the head with the tip of my thumb, massaging it as he massaged my clit. We were going stroke for stroke, moan for moan. My soft touch against his strong hands. My neck fell to the left as I envisioned him leaning over as he finger-fucked me while kissing my neck.

The smell of his Gucci cologne and the smell of his peppermint breath chilling my soul. I sped up my pace as my eyes squeezed tighter, sealing my fantasy deep in my mind. The pressure. The lust. Sweat dripping down my neck as the climax built to the breaking point. I moaned louder than I could control as my body tensed up. Cum squirted and sprayed the windshield like I was in a car wash. My legs twitched as my hand fell to my side as my climax subsided. My neck rolled as I bathed in the euphoric feeling. My eyes opened. I looked around and smiled. Never had I ever came so hard masturbating. I sat up and cleaned myself up. I reached in my glove department for my wet wipes.

As I was tossing papers around looking for them, a knock startled me on my driver's side window. I looked through the window into his eyes. No longer was he still a figment of my lustful imagination. No, he was now standing at my window.

Xzavier

It took everything in me not to chase after Sonja as she walked out the gym. I wanted to badly but I first had to let my erection go down first. That woman! God, that woman! She was something in-credible. In the beginning, when I first laid eyes on her, I just knew she was something special. But she ended up shooting me down. Only to force me to pick myself back up. I don't understand her, I don't. She was like a very difficult math problem with no multiple-choice answers. I just had to figure her out on my own.

As I stood in the gym, alone, my body ached to go after her. What we had just encountered was a mutual understanding with no words. Our bodies did all the talking. And the moral of the story was that we wanted each other. I shook my head trying my best to ignore my mind and body. My mind was telling me to go after what could be the best piece of pussy I could ever encounter.

And to make matters worse, my dick was still hard. That was called confirmation.

Fuck it! I thought to myself as I ran out the gym in the direction of Sonja.

As I was running in the hallway, I bumped into Ria as she was coming out of the restroom. Our chests touched first. I took a step back and excused myself. "I'm sorry, Ria. I was in a hurry and didn't see you."

Ria smiled and said, "It's okay. It's been a long time since a man has been in my path, and I actually liked it. "

My eyes diverted from Ria' s eyes, to her titties. Her nipples were poking through her bra. I looked away reluctantly, before they started to hypnotize me. Shyly, I rubbed the back of my hair smooth-ing down my waves. "I thought you were going to listen in on our rehearsal. Where'd you go?" Ria asked as she placed her right hand on her hip.

"I, uh, I was, but something came up. I'm sorry," I apologized.

"That's okay. You don't have to apologize, preacher. I tell you what," she said as she looked deep into my eyes. I'll give you a chance to make it up to me. Me and you, this weekend. We can go out, and I'll give you a solo session."

I was the king at speaking in parables, so it was easy for me to read between the lines. Us going out for a solo session wasn't just about singing. There would be singing, but she would be doing it from between my legs. That's for sure.

"Uhh, Ria. I..I can't," I said, more disappointing to myself then it was to her. I loved an easy catch. I was one of those fishermen that liked going to the lake before the sun comes up, set my line in the water, and settle for any fish. They don't have to be big, they all taste the same to me.

Ria looked at me disappointed. "Why not?" she asked.

"Uhh, because," I said, trying to buy some time to come up with a good excuse. "Uhm, because you're dating, Rudy. He's my best friend, I can't do him like that."

"Dating! Rudy!" She laughed. "I'm so single. Rudy and I are friends. He's just helping me get my career off the ground."

I nodded, but I knew Rudy better then she thought she did. Yes, Rudy might 've told her that he was going to help her get her career off the ground, but not before she let him pick her feet up off the ground, just to be carried over to his bed.

"So, what's your next excuse?" she asked sarcastically.

"That wasn't an excuse, Ria. I just don't want any drama in my life," I said.

Ria smiled. She walked closer to me placing her left hand on the center of my chest. "The other night, when we were all at dinner. You asked Monica a question. It was a question a normal preacher would never ask."

"That's because I'm not a normal preacher." I smiled.

Ria smiled then said, "Exactly. But, when you asked Monica to tell you something that she wished she could hide from God, I thought about what my answer would be if you were to ask me the same question."

"What was your answer?" I asked, really wanting to hear it.

Ria blushed, then she lowered her head. "I grew up," she started to say as I placed my pointer finger under her chin, raising it to where she was looking into my eyes.

"Whatever the answer is, don't be ashamed. Say it with confidence."

Ria smiled again as she rubbed her cheek against my hand as her eyes closed from my touch. Her cheek felt soft. Her lips brushed against my hand as she looked back up at me. For a second, I thought she would kiss my hand, but she didn't.

"I grew up in a church going home. My mother sung in the choir at my grandfather's church. I came up singing in the youth choir with Monica. I enjoyed singing, it was what I've always been good at. But I don't want to do it all of my life. Not singing in church that is. I mean, everyone knows Mary Mary, but they don't make money like the R&B singers do. That's why when Monica answered your question, I felt her. I too dreamed of making love to my own music. Is that wrong preacher?"

I shook my head. "No. I can't say that it's wrong. At all. A lot of things that we want in life can be accomplished without feeling that it's always bad, or sinful."

"But how preacher? Sex is considered a sin when you're not married, right?" she asked.

I stepped closer and whispered, "Can you keep a secret?"

She nodded. "Everyone sins, on a daily. I know that, you know that, and God knows that. I have sex all the time. "

"Really?" she asked surprised.

"Of course."

"But, how? You're not married," she said.

"I view every woman I have sex with as my wife. I love them all, as I love my neighbor. Marriage is in the heart, not the ceremony. Have you ever met God at the altar?" I asked her.

"No," she said shaking her head.

"Exactly, but the Bible says that we are all God's brides, right?"

Ria nodded and smiled. "Wow, I didn't think of it like that."

I nodded as I looked at my watch. I looked past Ria hoping I could spot Sonja, but she was nowhere in sight. "I'll tell you what,

Ria. I'll take you up on your offer. I'll meet you any place you'd like just to hear you sing. But you better sing your heart out, okay."

Ria nodded then she hugged me closely. Her hard nipples poked at my chest.

"Thank you, preacher. Thank you! And I will, I'll sing to you like you've never had anyone else sing before. I promise," she said as she backed away. I wasn't sure if she would be able to hold up on her promise because Monica blew my socks off, literally.

"Now I have to go. Go on and finish up your rehearsal. I'll see you, let's say, Friday night?"

"Friday night will be good. I'll text you the address." She hugged me again, longer then the first time. As we hugged, I shook my head. She kept calling me preacher, but I was the devil in the flesh.

As our hug broke, Ria walked back in the main church with a huge smile. I walked in the opposite direction after Sonja. I was hoping she wasn't gone for the day. I walked outside as the hot sun hit my face. I raised my hand to shield my eyes as I looked around the parking lot. I had no clue what kind of car she drove, but I was lucky enough that there weren't many cars in the parking lot.

I looked around. There were only ten cars in the lot. A few I had already knew who the owners were. I looked off in the distance at a Volkswagen. I decided to start my search there. As I walked up to the car, I tried to look through the windows, but they were tinted. I stuck my face close to the glass trying my best to look inside. I knocked twice on the window. I could hear something inside the car, a little rumbling. The car engine started, then the driver's side window rolled down.

To my surprise, Sonja was in fact inside.

"Hey, I thought you might've left for the day." I looked inside her car.

Sonja looked up at me with a half-smile. Her breathing was a little harsh, like she had just finished jogging. For some odd reason, I could've sworn I smelled a hint of pussy coming from her car but then again, I could be imagining things.

Sonja turned her A/C on and said, "No, I was just trying to get some fresh air, that's all."

Sonja looked up into my eyes, then she looked back down just as quickly.

"Sonja, there is nothing wrong with what just happened."

There, I said it. I admit I was a little nervous, but looking at a woman as beautiful as Sonja, what man wouldn't be nervous, even a little.

"What happened?" she countered.

I stayed silent. I didn't know how to put my thoughts into words without saying something sexual. Sonja was like a vein in my dick. She brought me to a hard point in my life without even trying. She was so hot, yet cold at the same time.

"Sonja, really. Are you telling me that you didn't feel anything back there in the gym?" My head hung as I asked the question. It actually came out wrong. I knew she felt something deep in her heart, but then again, I know she felt my dick pressed against her ass as we danced.

"What do you think I felt, since you know a lot, Preacher?" she asked sarcastically.

I sighed. I hated when I had to work for what I wanted. "To tell you what was going through your mind would forever be a mystery to my mind. But I can tell you what was going through my mind at the time."

A thin smile crept to her face. "Tell me what you were thinking then, Preacher."

"Okay. Uhh, as you danced, I could sense your place of comfort. Not the gym, or even the church. Just the simple fact that you had a beat, and someone to watch. When you started dancing, the rhythm of your body, the way it swayed side to side really made me think that you love your body, but more than love it, you praise it. You dancing was your way of thanking God for it."

As I finished talking, Sonja just stared at me not saying anything.

"Am I right, or at least close?"

Sonja burst into laughter. "No! You're way off. In fact, nothing you said made a lick of sense."

I looked at Sonja in shock. I was never wrong, never. I was able to read women like they wrote their life stories in my mind. But Sonja. Sonja was different.

Sonja wasn't like any woman I've ever encountered. She was bold, feisty, and enticing. She was beautiful, daring, and outspoken. She was a real woman.

"Sonja. if I'm so wrong, then tell me what's right."

Sonja stopped laughing instantly. She looked at me with a serious face.

As I stared into her eyes, she stared into mine, neither of us breaking eye contact. "Preacher, I can't tell you where you were wrong, because it was only your opinion. But I can tell you what I was actually feeling."

"Please do."

"I was feeling like I opened your mind to sin. And I don't like that. You stand for something, and I caused you to slip and fall. And for that, I'm really sorry."

"Ms. Echols, I told you, that wasn't your fault. It could, and would happen to every man that was in that position," I explained.

"And that's the point. It could happen to any man, but it shouldn't have happened to you, preacher."

I hung my head and sighed. I hated when people threw the 'P' word at me. It was like a weapon. And a curse. It was a title that I didn't want. A profession that I didn't earn, and I was tired of it.

"Sonja. If you'd let me explain." I held up my right hand stopping anything she was getting ready to say. "Yes, I'm looked at as a preacher. But first and foremost, I'm a man. Being a preacher has nothing to do with how I feel, or what I want."

"So, tell me, Preacher, what is it that you feel? Tell me exactly what you want."

"Okay, what do I feel. I feel that only because I'm a preacher people always and only look at my wrongs. No one cares what I do right, because everyone is always aiming to call me a fraud. I feel that I should be the last person to be judged. I know that I'm supposed to walk a straight and narrow path, because everyone is always watching me. But, if everyone is always watching me, then when will they ever notice that they are sinning too? That they are judging me like they aren't supposed to."

Sonja nodded in agreement.

"You asked me what I want," I huffed as I looked up at the sky. I knew the real judge was sitting above the clouds looking down on me with his eyebrow raised. He was the true judge, the one and only. Not even the angels could put in an input. I looked into Sonja's eyes. Inside of them, I was able to see myself. And looking at myself, I saw hope. True, real hope. Hope that I could one day be able to be myself, and not the man everyone wanted me to be.

"What I really want Sonja, is to be myself." I sighed. As the words left my mouth, it felt like a burden was lifted from my chest. No longer was the secret of the decade on my chest, but relief. And it felt great.

"What do you mean by that, yourself?" Sonja asked.

"All my life, I've been brought up to be someone else. My father. I was raised in the church, to take over my father's church. All my life I just wanted to make my own path. To wear my own shoes. To be me. But I couldn't, because of who my father is. Because of who my mother is. People look at them differently. They judge. Even when they aren't doing anything wrong, people still judge. They talk about us like we're the first family. But we're only human."

Sonja nodded. "I can understand that. You never really get any privacy," she said.

"It's more than that. I haven't been able to experience life as Xzavier. I'm always called, Preacher. No one cares what my first name is. Only thing that matters, is the word, Preacher."

"So, you don't want to be a preacher? You don't want to take over your father's church?" Sonja asked.

I smiled. She had answered the million-dollar question without me having to say a single word.

"Exactly! I love my father, and I love his church. I love the people that attend, but I don't have to be the preacher to love it all. I just want to start my own lane and stay in it."

"So why don't you?" she asked.

My head hung again, that was why I never told anyone the truth, because no matter who I told, once I told them, I would be still back at square one. "There's no way I could tell my father that I don't want to take over once he steps down. It'll crush him."

"So, what are you going to do?" she asked. She really sounded like she was concerned.

I shook my head then said, "I don't know. I guess ... do what I've been doing all my life."

"What's that?" she asked.

"Hold it in and do what any other good son would do. Take over once my father steps down."

"Wow. That's honorable, I guess. But if you don't mind me asking. If you weren't taking over your father's church, what did you want to do?"

I smiled. "I can't tell you that."

"Why not?"

"Because, you'll look at me differently. And I can't have eyes as beautiful as yours to look at me any different. I'm already blessed by God to have your eyes look at me if only for a second. I don't want that to change."

Sonja blushed. A strand of hair fell over her eye. She moved it out the way and looked at me. "How about this. If you tell me, I promise not to judge or tell anyone."

"I can't do that. The stakes are too high. But, how about this? If I tell you, how about you let me take you out."

"I don't date, Xzavier," she said calling me by my first name.

I smiled. It felt different when people called me by my first name instead of preacher. I liked it. I liked it a lot.

"We don't have to call it a date. We can call it a small gathering. A get together. Hell, it don't have to have a title. I just want to eat in the same place as you, even if we aren't sitting at the same table."

Sonja blushed again. Her beauty was immaculate. She made black women look pure. Her smile made me feel all gushy inside. "Xzavier, if I say yes to your gathering, this better be good. Whatever you're about to tell me better be something to make me say yes."

I smiled. "Oh, it's good alright."

"Okay. Let me hear it. And don't lie either."

"I won't," I said as I rubbed my sweaty hands on my pants. I had never told anyone what I really wanted to do with my life. I never even told Rudy, and I told him everything, almost. "All my life, I wanted to create people's fantasies."

"Like?" she asked.

"I want to bring people's sexual fantasy to real life. There's people around the world that dreams of making love to four or five different people at a time, but they don't want to be exposed, or judged. You have people that want to swing, but can't take the chance of getting noticed or judged for their actions. That's always what I wanted to do, bring people's fantasy to reality."

As I finished, I looked deep into Sonja's eyes. I looked and searched for a hint of judgement. A hint of doubt. For her to laugh or drive away. But I found nothing.

"Wow! Well, that one I didn't see coming," she said catching me off guard.

I just knew what would come next. She would judge me exactly like I said she would. "But," she said then paused, "we all grew up wanting to be something in life, even if it was as crazy as being an astronaut, or the president. I honestly don't see anything wrong with what you want to do. I really don't. What I want to know is, why haven't you done it yet?"

"I can't. If my father found out that I was doing something like bringing people together to have sex, he would have a heart attack."

"Didn't you say that you want to bring people's fantasies to reality, people that don't want to be judged, or their identity found out by the public. Right?" she asked.

I nodded. "You 're right."

"So, why not give yourself the same thing that you want to give everyone else? Get exactly what you want and do it without being judged. Get the fantasy you want, which is bringing others to reality, but do it behind closed doors."

As she talked, I was able to get a vivid picture in my mind of what I wanted to do. "Oh my God, I just got an idea," I said excited.

"What?"

"The name for the place I want to open."

"What is it?"

"Behind Closed Doors."

Sonja smiled. She honestly looked excited for me. It was crazy how I was able to get everything off of my chest to a complete stranger. Sonja didn't judge me, nor did she shoot down my dream. She actually uplifted it. And in the process, she gave me the name of my fantasy.

"I'm glad that I could help," she said smiling.

"Thank you so much. And I apologize for earlier. But I don't regret it," I said speaking the truth.

"To tell you the truth, I did feel something. But it took me deeper than emotions," she said bringing a smile to my face.

"Did you enjoy the feeling?"

"If I did, I won't tell you. I keep my fantasies in my mind."

Chapter 11
Sonja

As I drove home, I had a smile on my face the entire way. Today was actually a great day. What started off kinda slow ended with a smile. Honestly, I don't know what I'm getting myself into. I know I have a mission to accomplish, but I see myself getting distracted. And my distraction is none other than Xzavier. It started the very first day I laid eyes on him. The day I paid my tithes, the moment he said what he said. Telling me that I was the reason he knew it was a God. That set me off. The way he looked at me. It was as if he was seeing a woman for the very first time. But I had to keep my cool, even though he made my pussy steaming hot. I was there for a specific reason, and it was more important than having him get me hot and bothered.

But today, I saw something. I saw what I didn't want to see. I saw a man that was fragile from being tossed around so much, that any harsh movement, he'll break. But deeper than that, I saw a man that really liked me. I have a husband, that's no secret. But being married feels nothing like being cherished. My husband loves me. I don't doubt that one bit. But loving someone and being in love is two different things. Donnie, he loves me. But he's in love with his main addiction, gambling. Instead of taking me to a movie, he'd rather watch a horse race. When I want to go see a movie, or go out to eat, he'll go, but he'll be looking at the ESPN app the entire time, paying me no attention.

But Xzavier, he did more than pay me attention. He knew me without me having to tell him. Earlier he told me what he was thinking as we danced, and it was exactly what I was feeling. When Xzavier and I were dancing, I felt more than his dick on my ass. I felt alive. Xzavier was right. I did find comfort inside my body. I loved my body, and I loved a man that did too. I worked hard to stay in shape. I went to the gym on a regular basis just to keep my figure. It felt great to have a man appreciate it, and recognize my inner self at the same time. That's when I knew Xzavier would be a problem. He would be the only thing standing in my way.

"Hey, babe," Donnie said as he kissed me on the lips. I kissed him back as he closed the door behind me.

"So, what happened today?" he asked.

"I had a good talk with the owner's son."

"The preachers son?" He asked to be sure.

"Yes, the preachers son."

"And what did y'all talk about?" he asked as he rubbed my shoulders.

His hands felt great as he massaged my shoulders. All the pent-up sexual frustration has me feeling like I've worked a nine to five job.

"We talked about him following his dreams."

"What has he dreamed of?"

Donnie's hands were magical. I just wished his dick had the same affect.

"He wants to start his own business. He didn't say which kind." I lied.

"Isn't he supposed to take over his father's spot when his father steps down?"

I nodded as Donnie worked his magic. "Did you do what I told you to do?" he asked.

"I can't."

"Why not?" he asked a little harshly.

"Because Mr. King isn't that kind of preacher. He's really a God-fearing man. He didn't even look at me when I danced, I'm telling you, he's not like most preachers," I explained.

"Come on, sweetie. He looked at you. What's not to like when a man looks at you?"

"I don't know. He didn't though. But his son, Xzavier did."

"The next in line for the altar?" He asked.

I nodded. "Yes, him."

"How do you know he likes you?"

"Like you said. What's not to like?" My comment made him laugh.

"Okay. what did he say to you?"

"Today, we danced. I was supposed to show him my new routine I put together for the praise dance team. He came to watch. As I was dancing, my back was turned to him. Xzavier eased up behind me as I was dancing and started dancing with me, but on me. "

"And then what happened?" Donnie asked as he kissed all over my neck.

"His dick got hard."

"And what did you do?"

"I-I did nothing."

"When you felt his dick against you, how did it feel?"

"It felt good. It was ... big," I said as I moaned by mistake,

"How did it make you feel?" He asked as he sucked on my neck leaving a passion mark.

"It left me damp. I wanted to feel it. I wanted to hold it in my hands and squeeze it. To feel the veins run down it. To cradle it like a baby, but I knew it would be too big to treat like a baby."

As I talked, Donnie's hand slipped past the band of my leggings, and then into my already soaked thong. My clit was already swollen with lust, my sex lips dripping with its own drool. Donnie worked his fingers in my tight hole as he continued to suck on my neck. My back rested on his chest, holding me up as I squirmed from his touch.

"Tell me more," Donnie said.

"After I snapped back to reality, I ran away. I ran to my car, and I. . I. .. "I stopped the story. I didn't know how to say the words without hurting my husband's feelings.

"Say it. Tell daddy what you did."

I shook my head as he strummed my clit faster and faster. His fingers knew my spots."

Tell me, I won't get upset. Let me hear it."

A tear fell down my cheek as my legs began to shake. "I went to my car, and I played with myself as I visualized Xzavier's dick."

"Tell me about it."

"I pulled my leggings all the way down and then my thong. I spread my legs as wide as the steering wheel would allow me to. I closed my eyes and thought of him. I placed him in my mind, deep, deeper than anyone else has ever been. He was so far into my mind that I came all over my fingers. It felt real. Like he was actually there with me, watching me, urging me on."

"I love you, babe."

I cried what felt like a river as I came all over Donnie's fingers. I loved him. He was my husband. We exchanged vows. We had a ceremony. It was beautiful. But, why did I wish that I married another man. Xzavier!

Chapter 12
Donnie

I sat at the edge of our bed as I watched Sonja sleep beautifully, and peacefully. I loved my wife, but I knew she wasn't happy with me. It had nothing to do with her emotional state, because I was her shoulder to lean on and vice versa. It hurts to say, but the reason she's unhappy is because of our sex life.

I was born with a birth defect to my penis. To this day there is no cure, and no diagnosis. I just was born with a small dick, and it's still small. But what I lack in the bedroom, I make up in the tongue department. I have to say I'm a damn good pussy eater. I have to, it's what I use to make my wife cum.

When I first met Sonja, I knew she would be my wife. She was everything a man could want in a woman. She was amazing. Even after she found out about my birth defect, she still said yes to my proposal. I vowed to keep her happy and I've been slacking in every department.

Everything was going great, until I started gambling. What started off as fun and games, ended with me owing one of the most notorious Italians in the gambling scene. In the beginning, I had enough money to pay my debt, and I did. But I had a grudge with that poker table. I wanted every dollar I lost back. So, I kept going back, day after day after day trying to get my money back. Each day I went back, I lost more and more. What started off as fun, ended in a habit.

My first encounter with owing Fish wasn't as bad as the second time. The first time I owed Fish almost twelve grand. I took some out of our savings account and paid it off. That's how Sonja found out I was in debt, and in too deep. She forgave me, and I used her forgiveness as a crutch to keep gambling. The second time I owed Fish twenty-five grand, and I only had five grand left in our savings. Fish gave me what he calls, *The Lumps*. My face was so swollen when I made it home, Sonja barely recognized me.

She wanted to call the cops, but I begged her not to. Again, my wife forgave me. I made her a promise to not go back ever again to Outta

Luck. But I did. And to this day I can't tell you why. I was past addicted. Everyone knew I was addicted. That was why Sonja and I was I was in the predicament we were in now. In actuality, it's more me then her. I went back to Outta Luck thinking that I could control myself. I told myself that I was only going to take five thousand dollars, and if I lost it, I would leave with my head held high. Well, my plan backfired on me. I did only take five grand to Outta Luck, and I started off my night on a hot streak. I was doing great at the poker table. I ended up placing my last as my competition called me all in, but not only did he call me all in, but he also raised me another three grand. Three grand that I didn't have on me at the time. I could either call his bet or walk away with nothing. I had a great hand too. In my hand, I held two kings. There was a third king on the table along with two fours. That would give me a full house, kings over fours.

My opponent sat across from me with a huge smile. I gave him one back as I excused myself from the table. I walked in Fish's direction. Fish was an old school Italian with slick back hair that stopped at his shoulders. All he ever did was sit in the very back at his own table in his own little VIP section smoking on Cuban cigars with his bodyguards surrounding him. As I walked up to his table, Fish looked at me. He wore this thin smile on his face, one that I had grew to hate. He smiled only because he knew the reason for my visit.

I asked Fish to loan me another three grand. I told him exactly what cards I held in my hand, and I explained which cards were on the table. Fish didn't care. He only shrugged his shoulders and said that he didn't care. He gave me the money, demanding that I pay it back with a forty percent interest.

As bad as I wanted to walk away without his money, I couldn't. I knew fo' sure I held the best hand, so there was no way I could. I took the money, not gladly, but not with pride, just because. I could've quit playing when I was up, it wasn't about the money. It had become so much more. It was the chase. The hunger. The knowing you've mastered something that you couldn't do in the beginning. Just to say, I did that. That's why.

As I sat back at the table, I clinched my pride in my hand. The one thing that didn't really matter much to me. I sat my pride on the table, and it was quickly replaced with poker chips. It was amazing how they both meant nothing but shared the same necessity. My opponent looked at me. Not with the same smile he had when I walked away. This one was a staler look. One that I misread.

See, my opponent had mastered what I wished I had. I had misread his look with fear. Him knowing he would lose once I revealed my cards. But it was the complete opposite. His look wasn't fear, it was pure worry. My opponent was worried that I had become what I was trying so hard to avoid. Obsessed.

I looked at the dealer. She gave me a smile. Not that she thought that I would win. It was the same smile she gave me all day, even when I was losing. It was her job. But this time, I took her smile as if I was really about to win. My opponent looked at my two kings as I flipped them over. He shook his head. I jumped up and down as I saw his face. I began to scoot the large pile of chips in my direction. My opponent held up his hand, and for some reason it made me put a halt to my excitement. In his hand were his two cards. He stood to his feet and unhappily threw the cards on the table for all to see. My eyes were wide with disbelief. Two fours looked up at me as if they were in 3D. I was glad that my seat was so close, or else I would've fell down on my ass. My opponent even had the nerve to say that he was sorry as he dragged the pile of chips to his side.

Since that day, I've been chasing the same high with each hand. A high that never goes down. It's called pure adrenaline. To one day be one of the lucky ones to say I went to Outta Luck, and my luck changed. Yup, one day.

Xtasy

Chapter 13
Xzavier

Last night, I didn't get any sleep. I mean not a Z. I was up all night on the internet looking for a building to open up my own swingers' club. I couldn't get the name, 'Behind Closed Doors' out of my head. My conversation with Sonja really helped me in so many ways. She showed me that I was being a hypocrite, telling people that it was okay to have something you've always wanted, but denying the same to myself. That's why I called Sonja and asked her to meet me at my new location. Last night, I found a nice warehouse building that I could afford.

When I called Sonja, she sounded as if she was just waking up. She was surprised that I was calling her considering that she didn't give me her number. I told her that I got it from the directory guide my father keeps. She didn't sound upset after I told her. But she did want to know why I was calling her so early in the morning. I reminded her of our deal. That if I agreed to tell her my fantasy, that she would go out with me. My reminder caused her to laugh. I told her that I needed to show her something, and it had to be early. She agreed to meet me, even after I offered to come pick her up. All in all, I was just excited that she agreed to meet me.

I sat in my truck as I waited on Sonja to pull up. I had stopped by Starbucks on my way. I grabbed six muffins, and two white chocolate cappuccinos. I even grabbed a single rose just to show her that I was a gentleman. I was jamming the radio as I saw Sonja's car pull up in the parking lot.

I jumped out all excited, then I hid it that fast. I didn't know which one made me more excited, Sonja, or the new building. I met Sonja at her car door. I opened it as she smiled up at me. She wore her hair in a ponytail, a set of Prada glasses were pulled over her eyes. I held my hand out, Sonja took it and stepped out of her car. I stepped back as I looked at her. She was something serious. I wished that I had some glasses on. That way I would be able to conceal my eyes from staring at her so damn much.

"Good morning," Sonja said as she turned to grab her purse. I looked at her ass in her black shorts. She wore a white shirt that matched her black and white high heels.

"Good morning, I'm glad that you could make it," I said as she closed her door.

"I'm a woman of my word. We made a deal, so I'm here. And, plus I want to see what got you so darn excited to where you would find my number and call it at the wee hours of the morning."

"I did what you told me to do. I just wanted you here to see how a simple conversation of encouragement could change someone's life. I was up all night trying to find out what I really wanted out of life. And all I kept getting was myself. My true self. Not my father, or anyone's else version. Myself."

Sonja nodded as she looked through her glasses at me. Even though the tint was dark on the frames, I didn't need to see her eyes. I could feel her piercing stare.

"I-I, I'm glad that I was able to help. So, is this what you were coming up with. This building?" she asked.

I handed her a cup of Cappuccino as I took the lead. She accepted the cup as she raised her frames over her forehead. She took a cautious sip from the cup, and smiled after tasting it.

"I was looking at properties that were up for lease in this area. And this one stood out to me the most." I placed the key in the lock and opened the door to the warehouse. Sonja looked at me as I stepped inside.

"Wow, the property people already gave you a key. What, is this like a tour?" she asked.

I shook my head as I hit the lights. "No, I already bought the place. What do you think?"

Sonja looked at me in shock. "You bought the place!"

"Yes, I bought it this morning. Well, lease that is. I already gave them my first years rent, and I already got someone that's going to help me get my liquor license. I'm trying to have it up and running by the end of the month." I looked at my Apple watch and looked at the date. It was only the second week of the month. I had a lot to do.

"So, you just bought this place, off of a conversation we had yesterday?"

"It just any conversation. It was deeper than that. I told you something I never told anyone, and you gave me the only answer I needed. One without judgement. That's why I bought this place. Because there's people out there that need me. And I'm going to give them what they want."

I walked through my new establishment. I said the name in my head. *Behind Closed Doors.* Yeah. It was a bell ringer.

"People would come all over the world to get what I will be selling. I won't be selling people. No, they would be giving themselves away. I'll be selling something though. Fantasies. Whatever you can think of, I'll have it here, tucked away, and hidden behind closed doors."

Sonja looked at me as I stood in front of the bar. "You sound like you got it all figured out. Even with you creating other people's fantasies, what will you do about your own?" she asked as I looked at her mouth the whole time.

Sonja crossed her arms as she waited on my answer. I didn't have anything to say. I had a new fantasy every day. A woman could look at me, and if she is beautiful, I imagined I fucked her in a hundred different positions. Just because I know if I wanted to, they would let me. But I knew I had to keep my fantasies to myself.

"Each day, I feel like I'm getting closer and closer to my fantasy. So, I don't worry about it as much. But other people, they'll need a guide, an instructor. So, I'ma be the one to show them."

Sonja smiled. "Okay then. Since this is your vision, what am I looking at? Take me to this fantasy island thing you got in your head?"

"This area we're standing in, it's going to be the spot for the bed. I want it right in this spot. The biggest bed you've ever seen."

"Why a bed, and why right here?" she asked as she did a three-sixty looking at the floor.

"I had a dream once, and I was in a place like this. It was spacious, like this, and there was queen sized beds all around the place, but there were couches too. And in the very center of the room, was this huge bed."

As I explained my dream, I walked around imagining where I would place every item. Then, I stopped. I closed my eyes as I looked up at the ceiling.

"What?" Sonja asked. I could imagine she was looking at me wondering what I was stopping for.

"I'm going to place two poles, right here in this spot, ahead of the bed. I'm going to make it to where there is a handcuff on each pole. No, two on each pole. I want one for the wrist, and one for the ankle."

I opened my eyes as I looked at Sonja. "I wish you could've seen the dream I had. It was beautiful, sensual, and breathtaking," I said.

"I could imagine. But, I'm happy to say that I'ma be able to see it in real life. You're making your dream come true."

She was right. I was. The only thing was, when I did make my dream come true, who would I be able to invite? I didn't have anyone I ever told my dream about, so no one knew.

"I only have one problem."

"And what's that?" she asked.

"Who am I going to invite? I mean, how do I even get the word out about a place like this, while at the same time keeping it under wraps so people can come and go unnoticed."

"That's a very good question. Do you know of anyone that would attend that you feel would keep it a secret?"

I shook my head. "I'm not sure. I haven't told anyone about my dream, except you."

"I got an idea."

"What?"

Sonja smiled. "You could create a fake email, and email people from all over, even some that you know, like an invitation only party. If some people show up, then you'll create a few followers."

"And if no one shows?"

"'Then your secret is still safe," she said.

"It could work," I said tossing the idea around in my head.

"It will," she said then smiled.

"Thank you. "

"Let's just say, you owe me one."

"Whatever you want, just name it."

"I'll keep that in mind until I need it," she said as her phone began to ring. She reached in her purse and excused herself. I walked around my new establishment imagining where I would place each chair, couch and bed.

I saw everything as clear as day. I was going to make my dream come true. Every part of it.

Xtasy

Chapter 14
Sonja

"Hello," I said into my phone.

"You have three days to get me my money, or you'll be a widow," a male's voice said over the phone then the call disconnected.

I looked at the screen and sighed. That was the second call I received in the last two days. Each time the voice on the other end reminds me that time is running out. I almost called Donnie just to tell him that I had received another threat on his life, but there was no use. He had to have known, it was all his fault in the first place. My husband's addiction to gambling placed us both on the chopping block. And I was left to fix the problem. Or it would be til death do us part.

"Hey, is everything okay?" Xzavier asked. I knew my face was a dead giveaway. I felt like shit. Here was a man that was handsome, smart, and genuine. And here I was, using him, misleading him, for the greater good. But I had I had no choice; time was running out.

"Uhm, yes. Everything is great." I faked a smile as I placed my phone back in my purse. "So, what else do you see? Take me on your fantasy ride."

Xzavier smiled. "The bar will be over there. I want it to be nothing but high dollar liquor and wines. Vintage. Not cheap overpriced crap, but name brand expensive stuff. I want nothing but the best."

"What about a stage? Have you thought about if you wanted people to come and perform?"

"No. The only performing I want to be is people performing oral sex on each other."

I smiled from behind him. There was something about him that set me off. He was bold. he was daring, adventurous. He had no filter to his, sexual desires and I liked it. There was nothing sexier about a man. A man that knew how to really please a woman. A man that knew how to get a woman going without placing his dick inside. That was sexy at its finest.

Xzavier caught me staring at him. "Did I say something wrong?" he asked.

I shook my head. "No. In fact, you said everything right. X, when you're with me, I want you to know that you can be yourself. You don't have to pretend around me. You don't have to be a preacher. You can be Xzavier. The real Xzavier."

He smiled. "Thank you, not too many people would accept me in this likeness."

"I'm not most people. I know you look at me the same as most look at you."

Xzavier looked at me confused. "What do you mean?"

"You judge me. "

"No. I hate to say this, but you're wrong."

"I'm right. I know you judge me. You think I'm this super Christian. That I don't sin and think a little like you. But I do. Why do you think that I'm here?" I asked.

"Because, you want to help me get my idea off the ground."

"That, and because I'm one of those people that you're aiming to help. I have fantasies also, one's that I'm ashamed of, but still crave. So yes, I'm here to help you, but me helping you, is also helping me."

"What is your fantasy?" he asked.

"My fantasy is," I began to say as my phone started ringing again. I sighed as I looked at the screen. The bill collectors were calling again. I sent them to voicemail and blocked their number. I hated them damn bill collectors.

"Everything okay?" Xzavier asked.

"Of course. Now, where were we?"

Xzavier smiled. "Your fantasy."

"Yes, my fantasy. Uhm… my true fantasy is …" I smiled shyly. I had never told anyone my fantasy, not even my own husband. I mean, I told him what he thinks my fantasy is, but I had lied. I didn't think he would be able to take what my true fantasy was only because we both knew he wouldn't be able to perform it.

"I had this dream once. It felt so real. Kinda like yours, only better."

I smiled. "I was in a club, not one like what you're trying to make, but a real nightclub. I was sitting at a booth, and I was accompanied by another male. He was my date. My date ended up going to the men's room. While my date was away, a random guy. comes to the table and sits down beside me. He smiles at me with his hand under the table. He unzips his pants and shows me his dick."

"Did you know the guy?" he asked, into the story.

"No. I didn't."

"Then, what happened?"

"I looked down at his dick, it was close to nine inches long. The guy leans down and grabs my feet, taking my high heels off. He stands up, dick still out, stiff, and long. He walks to the other side of the booth, and slides in. I looked into his eyes as he started masturbating under the table. we locked eyes. It was intense. My date comes back from the restroom. He slides in beside me. My date and the random guy introduced themselves. Unbeknownst to my date, the guy across from me is slowly jacking off under the table.

Something inside of me rose up. Like it was born from down deep. I had gained a courage that I never known. I inched my bare feet across from me into this stranger's lap. My big toe touched his dick first. It was hard, the tip was sticky. I stretched my other foot out under the table. Somehow, I got his big dick between both feet and I moved my feet up and down in sync. The look on his face, it was … was …"

"Powerful," he finished my sentence.

"Exactly. I felt hat I was in control. The faster I moved my feet, the deeper his voice went as he talked to my date. If I slowed down, he growled under his breath. I controlled his body. His movements, his orgasm. I felt like I was …"

"God," Xzavier said, making me smile.

I nodded. "I felt like God. I had power in me that I never knew I had. It was amazing. Until…"

"Until, what?" he asked.

"Until I woke up." I sighed. I wanted to tell Xzavier about my husband so bad, but that would only ruin Donnie's plan. It was times that me and Donnie would be at dinner, and my fantasy would come to mind, and I would want to use my feet to jack him off. but I knew I couldn't. Well, not that I couldn't, but let's say that I wouldn't be able to. I knew my feet wouldn't be able to grasp his small dick.

"When I woke up from my dream, I wanted to go back to it so badly, so I could relive it. I to die in it, so that I could keep it as a memory. To have it forever."

"Fantasies are bittersweet."

"You can say that again." I laughed.

"If you don't mind me asking, why don't you have a man? You're every inch of beautiful and hella smart. You have a beautiful smile, with a perfect body."

I smiled at his compliment. "Who says I'm single?"

"Your conversation. The way you talk. I can see it written all over your face."

"Let's say that I have a boyfriend. Or better yet, let's say that I'm married. Did you ever think about that?"

"Some people can be married, and on the inside still be single. I know couples that attend my father's church. They stay in the same house but sleep in different beds. So, maybe you are married. But I can bet, if you are, you aren't happy."

"How you figure I'm not happy?"

"Because, if you were my wife, or my girlfriend, you wouldn't be here with another man telling him about your deepest fantasies."

I hid my smile well. "Okay, let's say that I was your wife, your woman, what would we be doing right now, right this minute?"

Xzavier stepped close to me closing the small gap between us. He was so close that I could feel the heat radiating from his body. I looked at his chest, then my eyes traveled to his face.

"If you were my woman, we would be in our bed, at our home, living out both of our fantasies," he said with a low, but deep voice.

My chest heaved up and down as I did my best to control my breathing. Xzavier's hand went up to my face. He caressed my cheek as his lips leaned in close to me. I closed my eyes, anticipating the taste of his lips, the softness. Just as his lips almost touched mines, I pulled back.

"What?" he asked, wondering what he did wrong.

"I can't. I mean, we shouldn't."

Xzavier sighed as his hand fell from my cheek. "What's the problem, Sonja? You can tell me."

I sighed as well. There was no problem. I mean, there was, but he wasn't it." There's no problem. I just…" I sighed.

"Sonja, I know you like me, and I know you know I like you, so what's the issue?"

"I'm not good for you. There, I said it."

"Sonja, you told me that when I'm with you, I can be myself. So, why do you have to be someone else? Tell me the truth. "What's stopping you from getting what you deserve?"

My head hung as he asked the question. It was the question that I had been asking myself for a long time now. Why was I getting the bad end of the stick? Why was I pretending to be someone else when I was actually a so much better person? But, as I asked myself those questions, the answers followed right behind. I knew why I was getting the bad end of the stick. I had married a man I gave my heart to, but I wanted to give the rest of me to another man. One I just met yet dreamed about my whole life. It was weird. I wanted what I deserved, but at the same time, I really didn't think I deserved what I wanted.

"Sonja, talk to me."

I shook my head. There was nothing that I could say. What was I supposed to say? That I was sent to his father's church to sexually exploit his father out of some money using the #MeToo movement. But instead of using his father, I decided to use him as the fall man. I couldn't. Why? Because he didn't deserve it. Any of it. He was so much better, and he deserved so much better.

I sighed as I turned to leave. I hated turning my back on him, but I couldn't let him see me cry.

Xtasy

Chapter 15
Xzavier

After me and Sonja parted ways, I walked around my new establishment with heavy shoulders and a fast-beating heart. My mind
was all over the place. I had a dream that I was trying my hardest to
make a reality. Then, in the other hand, I had a woman that I was
emotionally attached to, but deep down I knew I wasn't good
enough for her. Sonja was different from any woman I've ever met.
If she was still standing in front of me, I still wouldn't be able to
quite put my finger on what it was about her that had me on this
rollercoaster ride with no safety harness. I wasn't a rookie to beautiful women, but Sonja made me feel like a new booty around her. I
was fresh meat, and she was ripe fruit. Complete opposites, but we
went well together, like finger sandwiches and fresh fruit.

As I walked around imagining where I would place each piece
of furniture, my phone began to ring in my pocket. I sighed as I
eased it from my pocket. I looked at the screen as I read the sexual
text message from Monica. She texted me that she couldn't get what
we did out of her head. I sent her a quick text back. It was something
simple. A smiley face with his wet tongue hanging from his mouth.
As I sent the message, I wondered if Monica had any idea that her
so called best friend, Ria wanted me to make her feel the exact same
way, if not better.

I shook my head as I placed my phone back in my pocket. If it
was one thing that I really enjoyed, it was the ability to please a
woman. But deep down, that wasn't enough. As hard as I was on a
woman's vagina, I was even softer on their heart. In some ways, I'm
a player. But that doesn't change the fact that I'm still human. I was
in the game of sexual healing to please, not hurt. Yet I knew if Monica was to find out that I was seeing Ria behind her back, it would
break her heart.

My phone vibrated again. I looked at the screen again thinking
it was Monica with another reply, yet it wasn't. Ria sent me a text
explaining how she was looking forward to an amazing night, and
how she would keep me full an occupied the entire night. I knew

she was really ready for this night to end, so that she could get to tomorrow night. I knew for her, today was in the way. I went from doing God's work, to doing the Devil's work. From the healing business, to the heart-breaking business. And sadly, it felt good.

Friday Night

'I don't mean to come up selfish/but I want it all. Love will always be a lesson/ just get out of its way.' The Weekend smoothly blasted through the stereo. Whenever I was on my way to do the devil's work, I always jammed The Weekend.

He made doing bad things sound good and intriguing.

'I'm a prisoner to my addiction/ I'm addicted to a life that's so empty and so cold. I'm a prisoner to my decisions/ ohh-hhh!'

I was a huge Weekend fan. I had never attended any of his concerts, only because I knew my father wouldn't approve of it. But I did have all of his CD's. They were in my Wicked Song playlist. Each and every album, I would listen to them every day. All day long sometimes.

I took in every word The Weekend said as I parked in front of Ria's townhome. Her car was parked out front. The lights to her front rooms were on, the blinds were open, the curtains were pulled back, giving anyone with eyes a chance to see whatever it was they wanted to see from the outside.

I turned my car off and opened the door. I grabbed a mint from the middle console and placed it on my tongue. If it was one thing that I knew that could turn a woman off, it was bad breath. The other was bad teeth. I stepped out the car, closing the door lightly. My Mauri gators made the gravel sound under my feet. As I inched my way to the front door, Ria came in my sight in the front window. She didn't even notice I was in the distance staring at her. She looked amazing. I couldn't help but sigh.

The predicament I was in was the prime definition of a pimp in a hard place. I took the two steps leading in front of the front door. I knocked lightly. The door swung open. Ria stood on the opposite side with a smile sent straight from God himself. It was a genuine smile. A very happy to see me smile. And God was I happy to see her too. Especially with what she had on.

"Come inside, please," Ria said smiling from ear to ear. Ria led the way, giving me all of her backside. Ria was in her own home, but she was dressed to impress. The way her Chanel shorts gripped her round ass left nothing to the imagination. If she had on any underwear at all, Sherlock Holmes wouldn't be able to prove it. Her spaghetti crop shirt stopped at her navel, exposing the softness of her stomach.

"Did you find the place easily?" she asked as she led me to what I took as the living room.

"Uh, yes, I did in fact. You know GPS tells you every turn now-a-days," I said as I looked around her small, but nice furnished home. "You have a beautiful home, Ria."

"Thanks, it's small, but it's mine."

"You live here, alone?" I asked. I faced her as she sat down on the purpose couch, which in my book is the love seat. The love seat was a trap seat! It was used to seat people close, and comfortable enough to make a baby on, or in Ria's case, make love on.

I took the available seat beside her.

"Yes, I do. Monica used to be my roommate when we were in college. Then, she moved out. I've been here by myself ever since."

As she spoke Monica's name up, my mind and soul felt guilty in an innocent, I'm just being a man kinda way. I knew I was wrong, and that's what made everything seem so right. I had no title to what Monica and I was, and we never signed any papers stating we could enjoy anyone's else company, or pleasure so to say. I guess I felt guilty because they were the ones who were actually innocent. They just wanted something real, and for them, I was the next best thing.

Not authentic, but close enough. I was the figment of their imagination. The knight in shining armor. The strength to their weakness. The soul, to their mate.

"You say you and Monica are really close?"

Ria smiled. "Yes, we grew up together. We came up sharing the same clothes, doing each other's hair, everything."

The more she talked, the guiltier I felt about everything. But the look in her eyes, it showed me something. The look in her eyes showed me that she wanted me no matter what it'll cost either of us.

She already had a friendship with Monica. They were sisters in a sense. But what she didn't have that Monica had was me. The look Ria gave me said she wanted to share everything with Monica, like they always did. A family tradition.

"Ria, I'm a man, so me playing childish games will only shatter my morals. So, I have to ask you, why am I really here?"

Ria looked into my eyes, she reached out and took my hand in hers. It was more than a shock that traveled through our hands. It was as if we were made out of electricity. Like lightening had struck us at that perfect moment.

"Xzavier, Monica told me everything. And I do mean, everything. We have shared everything from a young age, until now. Some things never change."

"What all did she tell you? Enlighten me, please."

"Monica told me how you helped her bring her fantasy to life. How you made her submit, cracking her hard shell, just to show her how soft she really was on the inside. She told me that you made her sing until she came all over herself.

"And that made you invite me to dinner, for?" I wanted Ria to plant her own seed, and I be the one to water it so it would grow.

"Like I said, we always shared everything, even our fantasies. Growing up, we always fantasized about singing in front of millions of people. Neither of us being the lead singer, but both of us sharing the stage and fame together. And I guess that's why she told me to set this date up. Us together. Me, and you."

I was stunned. "So, Monica told you to invite me to dinner?"

Ria nodded. "So, what Monica and I did, it must've meant absolutely nothing to her."

"No, you're wrong, it meant everything to her. That's why she wanted me to experience it too."

"Experience what, exactly?" I always asked for specific answers, just in case I was being recorded, or set up.

Ria kissed the back of my hand. Her lips lingered on my hand as she brought it to her cheek. "Xzavier, she told me everything. How you felt inside of her. How you fucked her from the back as she looked out the window. She talked about it all the next day, and the day after. She went into such detail; it was like I was there. I could see you, entering her from the back. Filling her up as you sandwiched her to the glass. Her singing with her sweet voice, your deep strokes and the sound of your harsh breathing as you climax inside of her. I want that too. But, what I want, is you inside of me, for us to make our own memory. So, when tomorrow comes, I'll be able to talk of our experience with Monica for a day, or two. If it's that good."

My eyebrow raised as she said, if. "You said *if* it's that good. Do you think she lied to you?"

Ria shook her head. "I don't think she was lying. Even though we always shared everything, we didn't always like what the other liked."

I grabbed Ria by her face and hungrily kissed her. My tongue explored her mouth tasting the sweet red wine that she must've had right before I pulled up. As our kiss broke away, Ria wiped our juices from her lip as she tried to catch her breath.

"Maybe you're right! You might not like it like Monica did. You'll love it," I said as I kissed her again. I fondled her left twin in my hand through her shirt. Her nipple found my fingertips like a lost hungry dog. My fingertips pulled her nipple bringing a gasp from her soft lips.

"Where are you about to take me to?" she asked as she kissed all over my neck.

"I'm going to take you to fantasy island. Where all of your deepest fantasies will come true." I stood up in front of Ria. My dick was demanding to be freed from captivity. I stroked myself through my jeans letting her see what was in store for her.

"Is that all you?" she asked as she reached out to trace her fingertips along the length of my dick.

"It is, but tonight, it belongs to you. Every part of me is yours, and every inch of you belongs to me."

"Can I see it, please."

"You don't have to beg for what's yours. Own it, it's yours. Take ahold of it, get familiar with it, because in a moment, it'll be a part of you forever."

Ria looked into my eyes as she unbuckled my belt. She never lost eye contact as she unbuttoned my jeans. My jeans fell to my feet as Ria pulled my briefs down, exposing my dick. She took what belonged to her in her hand, weighing her options.

"It's beautiful," she said marveled at it' s size.

"So are you, "I complimented as she stared at her new prize.

Ria kissed the head at the same time she sniffed, smelling the erotic Versace cologne that I sprayed my body down with. "It smells, great," she said, kissing the head again.

To me there was nothing like love at first sight. The first kiss. Getting to know someone from the outside in. "You should see what he tastes likes."

"She. It's a she. You said it belongs to me. Therefore, I want it to be a she."

"Can I ask why?"

"Because it reminds me of myself. Soft, and gentle on the inside, but a hard shell on the outside. Powerful, yet submissive to the finer things in life.

"Okay, she can be a she, I guess."

I stared down at Ria as she got more acquainted with her new best friend." Monica had been replaced, stolen from her title. Swiped away like an angry husband at the dinner table forcing everything off the table, except for his own plate. Ria took her new bestie in her mouth. It was better than the first kiss. The tongue kiss was more passionate. More intimate. Ria slurped around her bestie like she was devouring a shell of caviar make from the finest chef in Paris.

My eyes closed as Ria sucked and bobbed her head back and forth. I wasn't trying to compare, but when it came to giving head, she beat Monica out by a mile. Ria sucked me and jacked me all in one motion. Pleasing her bestie, inviting her bestie to a place that was so warm, yet wet and inviting as a hot day in a warm hot tub filled with the most beautiful music, which was nothing other than her own moans around my dick. There was rap music, R&B music, and then there was soul music. When it came to soul music, Ria was the queen.

The throne was hers, and she wasn't giving anyone a chance to take her position. Ria came up for air, her lips glossed with her own saliva.

"How'd that feel?" she asked, smiling from behind her juicy lips.

"Words can't explain the pleasure I felt. But I can show you in so many ways what I felt."

"Are you inviting me to a good time?" she asked, blushing with lust.

"I don't have to send an invitation to what belongs to me, remember. Just sit back and let me get more acquainted with what belongs to me now."

Ria sat back on her love seat. The place she chose to feel comfortable. I took Ria's feet in my hand. They were perfectly manicured, polished with what I assumed was her favorite color, pink. Her nails had a sparkle on them. I licked the tip of the sparkle, making her shiver. Her big toe found its way to my tongue. Ria's eyes closed; a moan ran from her mouth demanding to escape from the pleasure that was building up.

"Ohhh, that's my spot." Ria moaned.

I shook my head as her big toe fell from my lips. "That's my spot. Every part of you belongs to me. When you moan, it's because I make you do it. So therefore, you don't cum until I tell you to. You understand?"

Ria nodded. She inched her hand down the front of her Chanel shorts. I grabbed her hand, placing them above her head.

"No touching what belongs to me, okay."

She nodded again. I knew the pain from the pleasure I was bringing had her body on fire. She wanted the fire put out; it was too much to bear. She was like me in so many ways. Even like her old bestie, Monica. We wanted the pleasures, even though we knew they could cost us our soul. We wanted to be free, knowing we could possibly be led to an eternal lake of fire. But the fire burning between her legs made the eternal fire of hell seem less scary. The only fire she was concerned about at this very moment, was the one between her legs.

I kissed Ria's lips as I unbuttoned her Chanel shorts. Ria eased up from the couch giving me the little assistance I needed to pull her shorts down and off of her. I stared into her eyes as I teased her sex lips through her thin Victoria secret panties. I might've been right by her favorite color because she a pair of pink panties to match her nails.

Ria humped into my fingers as I teased her sex lips while at the same time staring into her eyes, doing my best to find her soul, capture it, and claim it as my own. The front of her panties was soaked, flooding the thin fabric that was keeping my finger from finding the burst pipe. Ria opened her legs, inviting me to her Garden of Eden. I kneeled in front of her, her sweet scent was intoxicating. The sweet smell of her perfume, mixed with her erotic juices had me kneeling, praying that her pussy would be the best I've ever had.

I kneeled, bowed my head as I took in her scent. I looked, no, stared at her mound as I eased her panties down and off of her. Her sex lips were glossed, perfectly shaped, close together, waiting for me to separate them like a set of Siamese twins. I leaned forward, staring into her eyes as I kissed her juicy sex lips. I leaned back, her juices coating my lips. I kissed her trading her juices with mines. As I said before, I was hers, and she was mines, but there was nothing wrong with sharing.

Ria tongued me down, leaving not a drop of her juices on my lips, yet I still could taste her in my mouth. I was hungry, thirsty for more, so I went back for seconds. I wanted the leftovers, the crumbs. I was stingy with her juices, wanting it all for myself. I placed her left leg over my shoulder, my lips found her center, and I sucked on her hole like a honey suckle flower. She was sweet, better then honey, stickier than syrup, but damn she deserved to be poured all over a stack of blueberry pancakes just to be devoured and washed away with her juices. She was better than breakfast in bed. She was more like Heaven on earth.

"Ohhh, Xzavier. She wasn't lying!" Ria moaned as I sucked on her clit. Her body began to shake as I shook my head from side to side as I latched on to her button. I was in my zone, like a Pitbull at a dog fight. Nothing else mattered to me then taming her center, destroying what was in my path to walk away with the victory.

I raised her leg higher over my shoulder, reaching for the other leg. She placed her hand on her center. I leaned forward and bit her hand. She moaned as if what I did was out of lust.

"What did I tell you? Don't touch what's mine."

"But I'm burning. It's so hot down there. Please, put her out."

I shook my head. There was no water in hell, and no A/C in the ovens. She would burn, until I was ready to put her out. And I was just getting started. I grabbed Ria's other leg and placed them both over her head. Her sex lips smushed together, looking like the best beef burger a man could ever dream of. I mushed my lips with hers. My tongue slid through her slit, invading her cave that was deep and wet. I held both of her legs with my left hand.

I stroked my dick with the right hand, precum seeping from the tip. I gripped my hard dick in my hand and placed it on top of her swollen clit. I moved my dick along her pearl, the feeling was without words. My own body began to shake as the feeling traveled through my entire body. I wasn't inside of her yet, and she had me on the verge of climaxing. God's gift to man, a woman. A real, soft, gentle, sweet, woman.

I couldn't take it anymore. I was supposed to be setting her on fire, yet I was beginning to burn. I placed the head of my dick at her hole. Ria reached up to me, touching what belonged to her, if only for tonight so that she could talk of her experience for tomorrow, and if it's what she thought it would be, she'll speak of it the day after, and the next. It was my job to give her something to talk about.

Ria placed her hand under my shirt, massaging my abs with her cat claw pink fingernails. I pulled her forward. She raised her arms above her head. I pulled her shirt from the bottom, bringing it over her head. Her twins sat upright in her pink Victoria Secret bra. They matched the color of her lips. She reached behind herself and unhooked her bra. She pulled her bra down her arms and tossed it to the floor. She crossed her arms, hiding her twins as if she had just taken a bite from the tree of life finding out she was naked for the very first time.

"Don't hide what belongs to me. Let me see my blessing," I demanded.

Ria looked shy, like she was a virgin. I knew she wasn't, and the good lord knew also but there was a difference between making love, and just plain ol' having sex. There was a reason she chose the love seat. The couch with a purpose. Ria had everything a beautiful woman could want. But she was without Love. The one thing her God promised to give her. I wouldn't doubt she knew God loved her, but she wanted a love she could feel at the moment. A love that could penetrate. A love you can scream and moan at. Scratch and bite at. Nibble and tease. I loved what I do, but I hate it at the same time, I was sent to give love, temporary love.

Ria moved her arms, inviting me into her world. She was shedding her shyness, and replacing it with love, if only for the moment. Her twins were perfect. Not a single bump, scar, or blemish. Perfectly made. Mines, if only for tonight. I kissed her lips, trailing my lips until I found her left nipple. I took the point into my lips, softly pulling it with my teeth. I gripped my dick, placing it back at her center. I pushed inside of her tight hole, causing her to mean out her savior's name. It wasn't in vain, because what was to come next, only he could save her from it.

I slowly, gently eased inside of her. The feeling was pure, enjoyable, and satisfying. Ria stayed still, enjoying my girth, adjusting to it, making room for the rest. I slid in deeper. The entire time she stared into my eyes. No words came out, not a single moan or gasp. But a tear fell from her eyes.

As it slid down her face, I licked it away and kissed her with her tear on my lip. "Do you taste that?" I asked as I slow stroked her.

Ria nodded. No words needed to be exchanged.

"That was tears of joy, pure love. What you've always wanted."

She nodded again. Ria rubbed all over my chest and shoulders.

The look in her eyes told me that she was falling in love, but not with me. No, she was falling in love with what God blessed me with. For them, it was a blessing, but for me, it was a bittersweet curse. One that I wanted, yet disapproved of at the same time.

"Deeper, please," she begged as her eyes closed. I eased up on the couch, smushing her to it. I raised her legs over my shoulder and eased deeper inside of her. Ria' s cat claw nails scratched my back, leaving a scar, I was sure. A punishment for my sins. Ria placed her hands on my shoulder bracing for what was to come next. I eased what was left inside of her and sped up my pace.

"You feel so good, ma." I grunted as I felt her walls clam around my dick.

"You too." she managed to say as I sped up my pace. The couch began to rock back and forth. Ria's juices coated my dick as I watched it go in and out of her hole. That had to be my favorite part of having sex to a beautiful woman, with a pretty pussy. Just seeing what two people could do with their bodies was a work of art. Picasso couldn't have painted it if he was in front of us. A picture of what we were doing was better than an Oscar award winning movie. This was the definition of poetic justice. Passion, lust, and love. If only for tonight.

Xtasy

Chapter 16
Sonja

I felt horrible when I got home. My life had turned into one big lie, and for what, love. No, love didn't feel like a secret, and it damn sure wasn't a lie. Love was supposed to be pure, caring and safe. Not scary, and troublesome. This wasn't love, this was betrayal. I had betrayed a man that wanted nothing but the best for me. All for my vowels. For better, or for worse. Pshh!

"Babe, you're home," Donnie said as he met me at the door.

I kissed him on the lips. I searched for the spark that used to set me off, but it wasn't there anymore. Not even a little flicker. Nothing.

"How'd it go today?" he asked.

"If you're asking if Xzavier is falling for me, then yes, he is." I walked past Donnie to the kitchen.

"Sonja, is something wrong?" he asked like he was really concerned.

I slammed the cabinet closed. "Of course, something is wrong! You don't see it?" I yelled.

"Sonja, do you know why I have you doing this?"

I lowered my head. I didn't want to see his face. "Yes, I know why. Because you were more in tune with card games and a set of dice then you were in tune with me. What, did you love Outta Luck more than you love me, huh! Is that it, am I right?" I spat.

"No, Sonja! You know that's not true. I love you way more than anything Outta Luck could offer. You're my wife, my everything. You know that, don't you?"

"I knew it. But I can see now I was wrong," I said as I tried to walk past him.

Donnie grabbed my arm, stopping me in my tracks. "Sonja, I made a lot of mistakes, but marrying you wasn't one of them. I fucked up, yes, I did. I was addicted, and I went beyond my means, but that don't make me a bad husband."

"No, it don't make you a bad husband. But putting me into your business, and having me set up a preacher, now that does make you a bad person."

"The way you speak of him. He isn't a preacher, is he?"

I hated that I had even gave Donnie any ammo to kill Xzavier with.

"He don't want to be a preacher, but that doesn't make him a bad person." I defended Xzavier.

Donnie walked up to me. He wore a grim smirk on his face. "You have feelings for him, don't you?"

I lowered my head and shook it.

"Don't lie to me, Sonja. I never lied to you."

I stayed silent.

Donnie grabbed my chin and raised my head so that my eyes would meet his. "You're falling for him, aren't you?"

I nodded as tears fell down my face. This was all too much. I was sent to do a job demanded by my husband, and the only thing I found out was, that I was falling out of love with my husband and falling in love with the target.

"It's okay, love. I understand. I do, really," he said soothing me.

"You do?" I sniffed.

"Of course. Babe, you're beautiful, so I can imagine that he's reminded you of what I tell you all the time. He may be a handsome guy, who knows. But, it's neither of those things that made you fall for him. It's what he has that I don't."

"What does he have that you don't?" I asked.

"Don't make me say it, Sonja," he begged.

"No, since you think you know everything, I want to hear you say it. What does he have that you don't have?"

Donnie sighed. It took him a moment, but he said, "He has the ability to please you in a way that I can't. That's what I mean by I understand. But that doesn't mean you love him because you think he can please you. You love me. You always have. That's why you're doing what I asked. Because you know, if we don't get the money I owe, the man you love will die, and our love will fade."

The tears began to fall again. Donnie was right. I loved him. But love fades away like a rainbow. Donnie was my heart, my husband. The man I exchanged vows with, but I didn't sign up for this. Or did I? Was love a test? Was love a challenge? Was love even meant to run astray? because our love did.

I wiped my tears and looked into Donnie's eyes. "I'll finish what we started, but when this is all over with, I think we need to take some time apart."

"What. Are you serious?" He asked.

"Watch and see," I said as I walked into our bedroom. I snatched a comforter from the bed, and a pillow, and tossed it in the hallway. I slammed the door as my body slid to the floor. Donnie told me why I was doing everything. But I felt like Tina Turner. What's love got to do with it?

The Next Day.

Knock! Knock!

"Cone in," Reverend King said softly. I opened his office door so that he could see my face. "Oh my, what a surprise. Ms. Echols, have a seat. What can I do for you?" he asked as I sat in a chair across from his desk.

"I-uh. I want to ask you a question, or two. If that's okay with you?"

"Come on now, darling. That's what I'm here for. Ask away."

"I, uhm. I'm having trouble trying to figure out what love is. What's your definition of love?"

"As a preacher, I'm supposed to give you the Bible's definition of love, which is God. But you asked me, and not God. My definition is similar to God's in a way. Love, to me is seeing yourself, and everyone else around you in the best of shape and position you can think of. Love is subconscious. It's an emotion. Love comes alive when you feel vulnerable. Your body begins to accept the fact that hate doesn't deserve to be a part of you, so you lean on love."

"Wow, preacher, I never heard it like that before. So, basically, we only love when we get tired of hate. So, when I'm around a certain someone, and he makes me happy, it's only because I'm trying to find a way to get rid of hating someone or something."

"Yes, but no. I will say this. There is plain ol' love, and it's being in love. Being in love is when a person that you really care about is all that you think of. You toss and turn wondering what they're doing, if they're okay, and even if they're thinking about you. You pray for them before you pray for yourself. You will move a mountain for them no matter the size. Now that, that's being in love. When you plain ol' love someone, you can love them, and leave them. Yet you'll always in a way, love them still."

I nodded. Right then, I knew that I wasn't in love with Donnie. I just plain ol' loved him, and like Preacher King said, I'll always love him. But his son, Xzavier, I was deeply in love with him.

"Ms. Echols, I don't want to butt in your life, but are you having problems with the matters of your heart?"

I nodded, because I was having problems with the matters of my heart. I was stuck in the middle of if I wanted to just plain ol' love my husband for the rest of my life, or if I wanted to continue falling in love with Xzavier until I reached the very depth of what true happiness really was. "Yes, preacher. I really am."

"Do you wish to tell me what the problem is?"

"I umm, I have this friend that I've been knowing for a very long time. For years he's made me happy, and in a way, he still does make me happy, but I'm finding more and more each day, that the happiness and love is disappearing."

"So, what about the other guy? What does he do for you?"

"Other guy? I never said there was another guy."

"You didn't have to say it. When your words don't want to explain what's going on, the heart will speak up for you. The reason you're questioning what love is, is when you feel that love has betrayed you. Someone has come into your life and showed you a light that you didn't know existed. He's made you question what love is because whatever he's shown you, you didn't see it under the definition of love. Whatever he's showed you, it's beyond the form of words, like it doesn't exist. Yet it feels like it deserves its own meaning."

I smiled. Mr. King had hit it right on the nail. "I guess you can say there is another man, and yes, he has showed me a new meaning of love. One that I'm interested in finding more about."

"So, what's keeping you from finding out more?"

I was at loss for words. I wanted to tell him that I was a married woman in love with another man. And not just any other man, but his son. His flesh and blood. The next man in line to take over his podium. Saying it was on the tip of my tongue, but I bit it before it could come out. To do so was an ache that I felt deep in the pit of my soul. Lord knows I wanted to say that I was in love with Xzavier King. And I had a list of reasons why. His swag, it was perfect. His walk, masculine, but yet so particular, like he was moving on clouds instead of walking on earth. His smile, brighter than the sun, warmer than the blood running through my heart. His words, soft, yet strong and meaningful, pure, sincere. The way he looks into my eyes, as if he could see that I want him in the same way he wants me, if not more.

As bad as I wanted to say all of those things, I didn't.

"I'm afraid, preacher."

"Afraid of what, exactly?"

"Hurting one, or the other."

"By the pain written all over your face, it seems that you're the one hurting the most. If you have nothing else to give them other than the truth, then you're living a lie. You have to tell them. That's the only way you'll ever find true happiness, or you can ream in in the depth of this thing forever and before you know it, ten years will pass, and so will the opportunity."

I nodded. He was right. I had to tell Xzavier how I felt. I just had to find him, and the right time.

Knock! Knock!

A short, thumping knock sounded on Preacher King's office door.

"Come in," Preacher King said inviting the guest in. The door opened. Xzavier walked in with a smile on his face, until he saw me.

Xtasy

Chapter 17
Xzavier

Today was the grand opening of my first event. I finally finished decorating Behind Closed Doors, and I sent out invites to all the people that I thought would come and be interested in finding themselves. I sent invites to people that I knew who were they were. I got the idea from Sonja, who was a big help in giving me the push I needed to get things going.

Sonja, ever since the day she met me at my new place of business, I haven't stopped thinking about her. I know that sounds crazy knowing that I slept with Ria last night, but I only slept with her to ease her pain, not my own. The entire time we were entangled, my mind was on Sonja. I was a man, and I knew when a woman wanted me, yet Sonja had me confused. The way she looked at me, it was a tingle there, a spot in her eye that was only there when I looked at her. A gleam, a special place for me. But she denied me, again.

I was sure she liked me. I had no doubt. But then again, I felt that g was holding her back from what she wanted. What that was, I don't know. I was only hoping whatever it was would finally loosen its grip so that I could have what was mine. Something real.

I came to my father's office to tell him that I wasn't going to make it to the Deacon board tonight. I came up with a lie that I had caught a stomach virus or something and I was going to spend the next day trying to get better in time for Sunday's service. But as I walk inside my father's office, there she was. She's more than a she, she's everything she's supposed to be. But she was right there, staring at me as if I was everything she's ever wanted, but too far to grab.

"Father, good morning. Ms. Echols, good morning as well."

"Morning, son," my father responded.

Sonja responded, but it was softly under her breath.

"You're here early," My father said.

"I know. I uh ..." I stuttered as I had to shake my head to stop staring at Sonja.

"I came by to tell you that I won't be able to make it to the Deacon board meeting tonight." I stared at my father, but I could see Sonja sneaking glances at me from the corner of my eye.

"Son, you've never missed a board meeting. Is something wrong?" he asked concerned.

"I may have a stomach virus. It was something I ate. My stomach hasn't been right since yesterday." I told a bold lie that I know I'll always regret. But I couldn't tell my father that I was missing my first meeting because I was opening the doors to the city's first swinging club.

"Stomach virus. Why didn't you just call? You didn't have to come all the way here to tell me that. You know I'm too old to be getting sick, so you go home and call me if you need anything. I'll tell your mom to come by and check on you."

"No! I mean... I don't want mom to get sick either. I'm okay. I'll make sure I'm better before Sunday, I promise."

"Okay, son. You know the best doctor in the world. Make sure you pay him a visit."

I knew he was talking about God. I knew I couldn't go to God asking him to heal me of a fake stomach virus. I had way worse to ask him to heal me of. "I will father. I'll call you," I said as I walked towards the door.

"Good day to you, Sonja," I said as I walked out the door. As I was slowly closing the door, I heard my father say. "It's my son, right."

The Grand Opening
As I looked in the mirror in my own personal office, I asked myself if I was really ready for what was to come. Then, I began to wonder if people would actually come at all. I had sent over twenty people the invitation to come just to cum. I wouldn't be surprised if no one showed up at all.

I hoped someone did though. After all, I did spend almost every dime I owned fixing the place up. I did everything I thought a place of such caliber should look like. I had bottles of the finest wine lined up on tables. I had bottles of champagne on the bar. I had a custom-made flowing fountain of KY lube. Another flowing fountain of chocolate and over two hundred fresh strawberries. All I needed now was my guest. Oh, and to send an invitation to the only woman I really wanted to come. Sonja!

Sonja

As I stepped under the hot shower water, I winced as my body adjusted to the heat. I had the water steaming hot. It was my way of washing away my sins. I hadn't sinned physically, but when I saw Xzavier in his father's office earlier this morning, I've been dying to give him all of me. When walked in the room, my heart felt as if it had stopped, and then the second he looked at me, it started all over again. I listened to Xzavier as he lied to his father about him being sick. I knew the real reason why. Xzavier sent out emails to people inviting them to his grand opening, which was being held tonight.

I got an invite, and I wasn't sure if he meant to send me one. I was glad that I got the invitation. I really needed to talk to Xzavier, and the grand opening would be my only chance.

Preacher King knew how I felt about his son, it was only right that Xzavier knew also. Preacher King was a great man. I hate that he had to be a part of what was to come next.

I pulled up to Xzavier's place of fantasy. As I stepped out the car, a valet driver with a masquerade mask took my keys to park my car. There was no long line like there is at a normal club. In fact, there was no one outside except the valet drivers. Yet there was a bunch of fancy cars in the private lot.

I looked myself over once more. I fixed my pink masquerade mask over my eyes to conceal my identity and headed for the front door. I walked up to the bouncer and showed him my email invitation. He nodded and let me inside, closing the door as soon as I stepped inside. I looked around as I stood in the same spot in shock. The place looked amazing. Xzavier's dream had come true.

There were nice king-sized beds all around the room. Small love seat couches as well. There was one large bed in the very center with two poles at the very end of the bed. A large bar was at the very corner of the place. A beautiful Asian woman wearing a masquerade mask stood naked serving drinks. I looked around for Xzavier. I knew it would be almost impossible for me to find him with everyone wearing masquerade masks.

I knew Xzavier's dream was to bring people together to explore each other's bodies, yet everyone was standing around as if they were waiting for something to happen, or someone to come and tell them what to do. As the lights all moved over the large bed in the very center of the room, a man sat on the edge of the bed with a microphone in his hand. The crowd began to speak under their breaths as the man began to speak. I smiled. It was Xzavier.

Chapter 18
Xzavier

I looked around the room from my private office. I was beyond excited, yet I was super nervous. The place looked great, and the room was packed with guests wondering what they were really invited to. Even though everyone came with masquerade masks on, I could still tell who a few people were. Ria showed up looking like a sweet candy apple in her red Prada dress. Her masquerade mask had red sparkles all over it bringing out the red eye shadow she had over her eyes. I didn't invite Monica, but she showed up with Ria. I guess they really did do everything together. I looked myself over in the mirror making sure no one would be able to tell who I was exactly, then I walked out into the main floor to start the show.

"Hello everyone, my name is…" I hesitated as I remembered I couldn't tell anyone who I was. "My name is Xtasy. I know everyone is wondering what exactly is Behind Closed Doors. Behind Closed Doors is going to be my place, no, our place to unwind. This is going to be our private, secret, sex domain. This place is the fantasy island for everyone who has a fantasy, yet you can't bring it to life, for whatever reason. Most people call places like this, a swinger's club. In a sense, it is, but we're so much more than just a swinger's club. Some of us came alone, others with a- ·friend, or a lover. Whoever you came with, tonight they are not your friends, they are our friends, our lovers. We are here to explore the meaning of sex, the meaning of a one-night stand, the meaning of making love, if that's what you prefer. The drinks are free, the beds are clean, and the condoms come in all sizes. You cart leave now if this isn't the place for you, or you can stay and unwind. It's my job to make sure whatever you decide to do, it all stays Behind Closed Doors. Thank you, and I hope you really, really, enjoy yourselves."

As I finished talking, a few people clapped and some even whistled. I stood up from the bed that was roped off for the main event of the night and walked around. A man shook my hand and thanked me for creating Behind Closed Doors.

As he walked off, he walked up to Ria, wrapped his arm around her and walked he over to a love seat couch. I smiled, wondering if Ria knew who I was. I looked around as people began to drink from the glass flutes to get themselves more comfortable. As a naked waitress walked beside me with a tray of champagne, I reached for the only flute left, and at the same time another black woman reached for it. I picked it up and took a sip from it, then I handed her the rest.

The woman behind the mask smiled as she took a sip from the same spot as I had. "So, this is your place?" she asked with a beautiful smile right afterwards.

I looked at her as she smiled. I knew who she was. I could never forget her smile, even if I went blind. "You look beautiful Sonja."

She blushed and said, "Shh, I don't want anyone to know who I am. But thanks. You clean up well yourself." She spun around looking around from person to person. "Am I the only one that you noticed?" she asked.

"No, I was able to make out maybe seven or eight people. But I won't tell you who's who."

Sonja smiled as she took another sip from of the champagne. "I was surprised you invited me," she said.

"I was surprised you came. I mean, knowing what this place is and what it's all about, I thought you would just sleep in tonight."

"I umm, I came to talk to you about something."

"So, you came dressed like that, looking as beautiful as you are, while people are around doing any and everything to each other, just to talk?"

She laughed. "I guess that sounds silly right. But I did come to talk."

"Okay, so what do you want to talk about?" I asked.

"You asked me why I was acting the way I was acting with you. I guess that's
been on my mind, and the only way I could clear my mind, was to tell you."

"Tell me what exactly?"

"Do you remember when you first saw me, when I was paying my tithes?"

I nodded and said, "Yes, how could I forget?"

"That was the day I felt so invaded, yet beautiful. You made me want to experience what you were thinking that day."

"What was I thinking? How'd you know what I was thinking?"

"I knew because the way you looked at me. I felt as if my clothes were being stripped from my body. Your eyes, like how you're looking at me now. It made my body tingle. I can feel them, like a set of hands, roaming all over my body. Teasing me yet fulfilling my every desire. That's why when we were here the other day, I had to look away. I wanted badly to kiss you, to let you have me anywhere you wanted me, anyway you wanted. But I couldn't."

"If you couldn't then, why are you here now?" I asked irritated. *'Hey girl, what's your fantasy. I'll take you there, to that extasy. Ohh girl you blow my mind, I'll always be your freak. let's make sweet love, between the sheets. Ohhh baby, baby. I feel your love surrounding me.'* The Isley Brothers Between The Sheets softly played in the background.

It seemed as we kissed that Sonja's juices and the taste of the champagne from her tongue had me drunk, tipsy in her love. "Let me undress you, beautiful," I said as I climbed in bed behind her. I pulled her zipper down as her smooth, pretty, dark skin brought to my view. I kissed her naked shoulder as I continued to ease her zipper down. Sonja's head fell to the side as I continued to trail kisses all over her back. I eased her straps down her shoulder. People began to watch from a distance as I roamed my hands all over her body.

"Your hands, they feel magical," Sonja said as I walked over to her and stood face to face with me.

I smiled and said, "Stand up for me, I want to see all of you."

Sonja. stood to her feet. I grabbed her hand and gave it a light squeeze to assure her I was going to take great care of her, and her body. I slowly began to peel her tight dress from her body, kneeling in front of her as I pulled the dress to her feet. She wore a set of black pumps that I left on. Sonja stepped over her dress and stood directly in front of me. Looking at her at this very moment, I knew I would always have some kind of attachment to her, and it wouldn't only be sexual.

"Promise me something, X," she said, looking directly in my eyes.

"Promise you what?"

"Promise me that when the night end, you'll never forget it, and no matter what happens after today, you'll remember me as the woman you made love to, and not the woman I really am."

"This is the woman you are. This beautiful, free woman is you. I'll never forget this night, and tomorrow, if you want, we'll do it again."

A tear fell from Sonja's eyes onto her black laced bra. I kissed her soft lips to assure her that I was here for her. I wasn't just with her for the sex. I was with her because she was the only woman that truly knew me for who I really was. Sex with her would just be the icing on the cake.

As our kiss broke, Sonja reached behind her back and unhooked her bra. She let her arms fall at her side. Her bra fell to the floor beside the empty glass flute. The same glass flute that gave her the courage to give her entire being to me.

"Lay down for me. Let me ease whatever it is that's on your mind. Place me at the front of your mind, make me your main focus. Let me be the center of your attention. Ignore everything, the people around us, and what's to come tomorrow. For right now, it's just us. This is our moment, our night. Okay."

Sonja nodded as she laid on her back. Her twins bounced as she got herself comfortable on the soft white sheets.

I removed my suit in record timing. I was anxious to feel the inside of her. I stood before her in only a pair of boxer briefs. My dick was hard pressed to get out. Like he could feel the heat radiating from her body, the trigger to set him off.

I crawled on my knees across the bed to her. I could see the dampness on the crotch of her panties. Sonja opened her legs, inviting me into her warm, loving home for the very first time. I wanted to make a great first impression, just so she would invite me back for a second visit. I crawled between her smooth chocolate thighs as they laid sprawled open, waiting for me to hold them tight. Sonja smelled as if she had invented perfume. She smelled just that good. I closed my eyes, inviting her scent into my mind, storing it away for a later time, just in case this would be my only time with her. A memory I never wanted to forget.

The anticipation was killing me. I wanted so badly to speed up the process of foreplay just to feel the insides of her walls, but I knew patience was a virtue. If you wanted something done right, you had to take your time with it. So, took my time I did.

Sonja looked down at me, but she didn't see pity, and she damn sure wasn't disappointed. What she saw was the look in my eyes. She saw death in my eyes. She knew I was about to kill her pussy. She laid her head flat on the bed as I slid her panties to the side. The way her panties split between her pussy and ass cheeks was a beautiful sight. Her sex lips were perfect, bald, juicy and pink. I kissed them, just a peck. I wanted to get acquainted with them to know it's wants, likes, and needs. This was personal.

Sonja's back raised from the bed. She was possessed by my tongue. I slid the tip of my tongue across her slit, then up and down like I was trying to catch a drop of ice cream from falling. She tasted sweet, like strawberry ice cream. Sticky, and slippery, like my hot tongue was melting her. I gripped the bottom of her thigh, pulling her close to me so I wouldn't have to chase my food.

"Close your eyes. Take yourself to your fantasy. Open your mind, free your wants, and let me give you exactly what you need," I said as I dove face first into her sweet nectar. Soft moans, mixed with oohs and ahhs filled the air as a crowd of spectators looked and stared at me eat my food with no hands.

I used my thumb to tease Sonja's clit as my tongue did the dirty work. A woman laid down beside Sonja in the opposite direction. An unknown man laid on top of her as they kissed to the sounds of Sonja's moans. The man raised the woman's dress. She was completely naked underneath. As my tongue gave Sonja a cavity search, my eyes watched the woman and her mystery man start their fantasy. The woman leaned forward as the man took her dress over her head. Her titties were nice, tanned and pointy. The man grabbed her under her arms and pulled her closer to him. He roughly sucked on her twins, going from left to right as the woman ran her hand through his waves. I was into their love session, but I never missed a step in my tongue tango with Sonja's sex lips.

The man behind the masquerade mask unzipped his pants. He was too anxious to get completely naked, or maybe he had his own complex about being naked in front a room full of strangers. The man slid his hard dick out of his zipper slit, the woman opened her legs wide and raised them in the air as if she was doing a leg workout. The man leaned forward and kissed her passionately as she gripped his dick and eased it inside of her wet hole. The woman gasped. Her head turned to the side, facing Sonja. The woman reached over and caressed Sonja's tears away. Sonja opened her eyes and looked at the woman. The woman was staring into Sonja's eyes with her mouth gaped open as the man fucked her hard and deep. Sonja pulled the woman to her and kissed her passionately. That was all I needed to see.

I wiped Sonja's juices from my mouth as I eased my briefs under my hard dick down to my knees. I didn't take Sonja's panties all the way down. I wanted to fuck her in the costume she chose to wear. I listened to The Isley Brothers as I lined my dick up with Sonja's wet entrance.

'Ohh, I, like the way you receive me/ yeah I love the way you relieve me.' The Isley Brothers sang.'

As I eased inside of Sonja's super tight box, I was forced to look down at her. She broke her kiss off as it felt like I had broken her barrier and made her a woman all over again. She was tight, hot and breathtaking. I had never had a woman whose walls gripped my dick like it had done something wrong. Her walls snatched and grabbed, holding my dick tight, squeezing it, like it had upset her walls.

I leaned forward and kissed under Sonja's eyes. She leaned her head back. I gripped the firmness of her neck, tracing my thumb up and down her throat. I kissed her juicy lips as she humped up into me. I didn't pay much attention to the couple next to us. I was too busy staring into Sonja's beautiful eyes. She was everything that I expected her to be and so much more. The way she danced in the church's gym, I knew her rhythm was something special.

We danced close together on the bed as another couple did the same. Our bodies moving in sync creating a masterpiece for all to see and want to mimic.

"From the back," Sonja said as she looked into my eyes. I nodded as I eased my dick from her tight hole. Sonja rolled over on her stomach.

As she did, I took a look around the room. There were people making love all over the place. Some were still looking at Sonja and I make love. There was a man sitting in a chair, and as he stared at us, a woman was on her knees in front of him giving him head. What started off as a stale kick back, ended up being everything I always wanted.

I stared at Sonja's backside as she bent over, on her knees, anticipating my entrance into her world. Her sacred place. Her flower blossomed from between her legs, wet from the morning dew, yet still beautiful. Her scent was definitely a rose, layered into perfection. I teased her folds with my middle finger, gaping a hole. As I eased my finger from her slippery tunnel, her hole closed like I was never there. Beautiful. Amazing, and worth the wait.

"Do you see how everyone is watching us," I said as I gripped my dick and lined myself up with her hole.

Sonja nodded as she looked over her shoulder at the star witnesses of her fantasy. Something she's always wanted. "This is amazing. Your dream is what everyone else considered a nightmare. Lust is beautiful," she said as I eased inside of her slowly. Sonja moaned as I pushed past her tight walls to the hilt. I held my position like my commander had commanded me to. Sonja moved slowly into me, rocking back and forth like she was trying to put my dick to sleep. The motion she used; it was like she was dancing inside a hoola hoop. Her hips moving in a circular motion, grinding if I may say so. I closed my eyes as I enjoyed her making love backwards to my dick. The sounds of our love making were loud as it mixed with other couples' moans. Even though the rules stated no one could bring their phones, I wished I had a camera. This was a moment I wanted to relive over and over. I gripped Sonja's juicy ass as she rocked back and forth into me. I never rocked my hips once, I let her do all the work, and she was putting in overtime. My balls tightened under me as the pressure became too much to bear. It was time. Time for Sonja to clock out. A job well done.

Chapter 19
Sonja

I was in a trance like state as Xzavier eased his stiff dick inside of me. Xzavier had the type of dick game that made you want to be high while he was inside of you. He made me feel sexy, desirable, wanted, amazing. He never moved as I rocked into him. He let me take control, make all the moves, yet I felt his dick move on its own. With Donnie, he did all the work, and I never felt a thing. With Xzavier, I felt him hit every wall, with every stroke. His dick had a mind of its own. He was a savage when it came to having sex. Dominant, yet submissive to my body. Gentle, yet rough when he wanted to be.

"You feel that daddy?" I asked as I felt his mushroom head grow inside of me. He never said a word, but I knew he felt it. I knew he felt me. And I felt him too.

"You're amazing," he said as he leaned over and kissed my back. His kiss was gentle, caring. I've heard women say that they've fell in love with a man's dick. And I was a living witness. I was head over hills in love with this man's dick. The length, the girth, even the veins. The blood flowing through them.

It was all so powerful, so real. This was no longer a fantasy I was living out; I was alive. I was attached, and I never wanted us to separate. But all good things must come to an end. And the end was near, I could feel it pushing through my insides. The power of his explosive semen pushing its way inside of me. We didn't have any protection on, and I still felt safe with him. As he came inside of me, I came as well. My knees grew weak, but my motions never stopped as I continued to rock back and forth slowly into him.

Xzavier grabbed me by the hips and held me steady. I knew he had come to a sensitive moment. I could feel his semen as well as my own seeping down my sex lips. Xzavier eased out of me. He held me steady as he leaned forward and kissed my ass cheeks. He used his right hand and rubbed the base of my pussy, smearing our juices all over my sex lips, moisturizing them. My head fell forward.

My hair fell over my face. I was glad that it did. I didn't want anyone to see my facial expression. The look of love. The look of submitting to one's penis. I wasn't ashamed, just nervous. I was nervous of what was to come next. What was to come after two people that didn't mean anything to each other cums. The post sex syndrome.

I turned around and sat on the bed. Xzavier panted as he did the same. A loud applause came right after. People cheered us on, whistled as we tried to gather ourselves. I looked around the room. People were naked, enjoying the view. I didn't bother to cover myself. Everyone had already had their eyes full. I looked at a man that was standing not too far off at the bar. He looked at me with a masquerade mask on. He held my stare as he smiled from ear to ear. Even though he had on a mask like everyone else, I knew his eyes from anywhere. Just seeing Donnie stare at me after I had just had sex with another man made me feel uncomfortable. I snatched the sheet from the bed and covered myself with it. Xzavier looked at me wondering what was wrong. Yet, I couldn't tell him that my husband had crashed our love session, and only God knew what he was up to.

"Sonja, what's the matter?" Xzavier asked as he placed his hand on my shoulder.

I flinched under his touch. Tears streamed down my face as I stood up and ran away. I didn't look back as Xzavier called after me. I ran right past Donnie and his big stupid smile. Behind Closed doors had finally been opened.

***

Donnie

I watched from a distance as Sonja really really enjoyed herself. She was so caught up in Xzavier's dick game that she didn't even know I was there, watching her take his dick like a champ. As she rocked back and forth into him, I found myself getting a little jealous. I wasn't a homosexual, but he had me beat in the dick department by a few inches. My plan was working; but it didn't feel good at all. I loved my wife. She was my everything, my world. I wasn't supposed to be sharing her with a man that was able to fulfill her every need. I wasn't supposed to be using her like a pawn, but even love was all a game. It was a game that was often played, but no one really knew the rules.

Our marriage was for better or for worse, and this was the worst I think it could get. Even though I set everything up, it still felt like she was cheating on me. My plan was simple, all she was supposed to do was come her and let him have her in any way he wanted while I sit back and record everything. Even though I left the recording part out, and me coming to watch part. What made it all so bad, I could see the look in Sonja's eyes as they had sex. It was love. The way she looked as she rocked back and forth into him; it was the same way she looked at me when we said I do. Pure love. She loved the man that was deep inside of her wet pussy. She loved the way his dick felt. She loved the way he gripped her ass. She loved the way he let her take control. She loved the way he let her rule her fantasy. To be the queen of the show, the head bitch in charge.

As Sonja rotated her hips into him, I saw his eyes close. I knew what he was feeling. It was the same way I felt when she did it to me. The world seemed to stop moving. The stars seemed just a little bit brighter. The moon looked bigger. No pain was there. The world seemed perfect.

Joy seemed to take over your mental, and your body seemed to be high off of the greatest weed ever grown. I knew he felt like he was in another dimension, another galaxy. A planet that always makes you feel like you can do anything. A planet that makes you feel like nothing else matters except getting your nut. A planet that makes you cum to your senses. I watched as Xzavier held her steady, using her hips to balance him. A soft crutch that you can grip and squeeze. A crutch that a man wasn't afraid of holding on to.

Sonja's movements stopped. She had cum to her senses too. Neither of them moved for a second or two, they just stayed there, joined together like holy matrimony. Stuck in their fantasy, never wanting it to end. But all things must come to an end. Xzavier eased his dick from her slippery hole. I then noticed that he wasn't wearing any protection. That he had went bare back inside of my wife, and left her with a sticky parting gift. Sonja slowly sat down as she did her best to gather herself. Xzavier did the same. The room fell silent as everyone looked at the couple in the center of the room that had just made a statement. A statement that said, sex is more than just sex, it's magic. I began to slow clap as I stared at them. I didn't do it for my benefit, I did it for them. They had both did what they came here to do. They both got what they wanted, and so did I.

I tucked my iPhone in my pocket as Sonja looked up at me. She looked directly at me as if she knew who the man behind the mask was. I smiled at her. I was proud of her, even with the anger growing inside of me. She did what I wanted her to do, and in return she got everything she needed. It was a win-win situation, but somehow I still felt that I had lost something.

Sonja began to cry as she looked at me. I had a smile on my face as I held it in place like the mask that was covering my eyes. I didn't want her to feel that she had done anything wrong. I wasn't hurt by her actions. I was hurt by my own. To sacrifice a specimen so beautiful, so pure, for my own selfish greed. I deserved to lose her, no matter how hard I was willing to fight for her. He had won, just for tonight.

Sonja snatched the sheet from the bed and covered herself with it like I was seeing her naked for the very first time. She stood up and ran as Xzavier called after her. She never looked back, nor did she look at me as she sprinted out the front door. I looked at her as she left Behind Closed Doors wide open.

Chapter 20
Sonja

I heard the front door open and close as I lay in bed eating a pint of red velvet ice cream. The TV was on, and a great movie was playing on the Oprah Winfrey network. The story was similar to my own. It was about a woman that was stuck in a relationship she had committed herself to, yet there was a man that she wanted to recommit herself to. Tears streamed down my face as Donnie walked into the room as he held a smile on his face. The same smile he wore when he saw me in Xzavier's fantasy island. an island that I wished I was stranded on with just me and Xzavier. No one else, no bartenders half naked, no crowd of freaky nervous spectators, just me Xzavier, and his large bed.

I looked at Donnie's smile. It was the same smile that brought me back to reality at Xzavier's place. The sick reality that Donnie and I were throwing on Xzavier and his family.

"Why are you crying, babe?" Donnie asked as he sat at the side of his bed.

The same side that he made warm at night when I was cold. If only he could warm the coldness of my heart. The vacant spot that was once held only for him.

I wiped my tears and sat the ice cream on the nightstand. I sat up in bed and brought the sheet over my chest. "Why were you there tonight?" I asked.

"I was enjoying the show like everyone else," he said as he kicked off his shoes.

I grilled him as he began to take off his shirt. I turned my head as I caught myself staring at his abs. He was physically beautiful in the ugliest way. I used to shiver at the sheer sight of him, now I wished I could undo him, the memories, and the love. I don't wish to hate him, because hate is such an ugly word, but I wish that I could dislike him in the most romantic way.

I was in a depressed stage; stuck in between my marriage and a love affair that I was pushed into.

"You never told me that you were going to go. If you would've told me you were coming, I wouldn't have done it."

"Exactly. That's why I didn't tell you. It was the only way I could go and record everything and you look and enjoy yourself in the way you did."

"Record! Please tell me that you didn't record what happened tonight." I was upset, and I felt betrayed. The plan was simple, yet he made it complicated.

"I did it for proof."

"Proof, which wasn't the plan. The proof was supposed to be his semen inside of me, not a film for all to see." My words took Donnie's smile away, and I was happy for it.

"I made proof because a little semen in some little pussy wouldn't be enough evidence," he spat.

"Oh, so now I'm just some lil pussy," I scuffed then said. "Okay, you know what, I'm out." I stood up and slid my feet into my pink Chanel house slippers.

I grabbed my car keys as the tears began to betray me again. There was something about turning your back on a man you pledged to always have back. But I was strong, or at least I claimed to be.

"Where are you going?" Donnie asked as I started for the door.

"I'm going to let the truth sink in so I won't feel like I'm living a lie."

Donnie didn't say a word as I placed my hand on the doorknob. He didn't beg me to stay, or ask to go with me. I was always told that if you love someone, you'll fight for them, yet Donnie didn't even put up a struggle. He didn't break a sweat.

Xzavier

There was nothing else I wanted to do at the moment then to talk to Sonja. For some, the night was a complete success. Some people were finally able to come out of the hiding they had place themselves in and be free. They were no longer ashamed of who they were on the inside, and they finally let it show tonight on the outside.

What was supposed to be a complete success for me, ended up in a failure. I came a long way with Sonja, and when I say we came, we did cum. But somehow, she still ended up in tears. When I was breaking her barrier down, knocking her every wall down with every stroke I took, her moans let me know I was going to be victorious. And after every brick that fell, after every wall that collapsed, her floodgates opened, and she came to her senses. This wasn't just a war from the inside, it was a war on the outside.

On the inside, she felt that we were joined together like Siamese twins, but on the outside, her reality was the only thing keeping her from living in her fantasy. Something was holding her back, keeping her down so she wouldn't rise to the occasion with me.

I was now at home drinking a glass of Patron to ease the bliss she left me in. I just didn't understand it. I thought we shared a moment together.

Then, I realized that when you share a moment with someone, that's as long as it'll last, a moment. Why couldn't a moment last a lifetime? Why couldn't it be like a memory, where I can pick up when I felt like it. Cherish it when I wanted to, and use it for a crutch when I felt down. Use it for happiness when I felt sad. But a moment only lasts a moment.

Soft music played in the background as I tried to relive the moment I shared with Sonja. The feel of her soft skin slapping against mines. The way her mouth felt over mines. It was a moment worth renewing. A moment worth reliving. I wish life had a rewind button like the movie Click. I'd rewind our moment a make it a lifetime until the battery runs dead. Then, I'd die in the moment happily.

A knock came at the front door. I scoffed as I was brought back to reality, a place that I no longer wanted to live in. I paused the music as I went to answer the door. I looked through the peephole and to my amazement it was Sonja. I pinched myself to make sure I wasn't living in a fantasy, that this was actually my reality. I know I said before that I no longer wanted to live the reality life, but I lied. I wanted to live anywhere Sonja was living. She could be in hell, and we'll still be together, no matter how hot the flames were. We could live in Heaven, and Lord forgive me, I'll be praising her instead.

I opened the door as Sonja stood on the other side with her arms crossed. Her makeup was smeared, and her eyes were red. She wore a housecoat and a pair of house slippers.

"Sonja, what are you doing here?" I asked. It was the only thing that came to mind, even though I was happy to see her.

"Can I come in? I really need to talk to you about something."

I stepped to the side as she walked in. I closed the door behind her and locked it. I walked behind her, staring at her shape as it molded into her housecoat. It was only hours ago I was inside of her. The nicest place on earth.

"Is something wrong?" I asked her. She didn't say a word. "Okay, umm, would you care for a shot of patron, or some water?" I offered.

"Patron would be great, no ice please."

I nodded as I went to grab her a glass. I watched her from the bar as she toyed with her fingers. I had always known something was eating her up on the inside, but I never expected whatever it was to eat its way to the outside.

I sat beside Sonja and poured her a double shot of Patron, then I refilled my own glass. I handed her the glass. She never looked up at me as she accepted it and took half the shot to the head. I knew it burned, but whatever it was that was bothering her burned way worse.

"So, umm," I said, unsure of what to say next. "What did you have to talk to me about?"

"There's something that I need to tell you. Something that I should've been told you a long time ago."

I sat my glass down on the table and faced her for the news that had her in distress. "Tell me. Whatever it is, I know we can fix it."

"I don't think so. Everything just can't be fixed," she said.

"It can, as long as you got the right tools to get the job done."

She sighed and took another sip from her glass. "I'm married, Xzavier," she blurted out like the words didn't want to come out.

I sat back on the couch and nodded as her statement sunk in. She wasn't the first. woman I had sex with that was married. But she was the very first woman I made love to that was married. Her being married wasn't the worst problem. It was her being married and I wanted to be her husband, that was the problem. I was in love with a married woman. The only thing I wanted to know was if she still loved him.

"Do you love him?" I asked as I hoped she would look into my eyes and tell me the truth.

She nodded and said, "Yes, I do. He's my husband. I married him because I loved him. But, that's not the worst thing I have to tell you."

I looked at her wondering what could be worst then having sex with another man while she's married. I knew she couldn't be pregnant because we only had sex once, and that was only a few hours ago.

"Sonja, you're here to put everything on the table. Don't just give me half of the news, and hide the rest in a napkin."

"I can't," she said as she started crying.

I grabbed her hand and held it in mine. "You can tell me. What's on your mind, let it all out."

Her phone chimed in her hand as she opened her mouth to speak. She looked at the screen and huffed as she opened the message that was sent to her. Whatever it was made her cover her mouth. She closed out the message and tossed her phone on the table.

"What was all that about?" I asked.

"Never mind that," she sighed. "Can I have a refill?"

"So, you're not going to tell me what's bothering you?"

"No. I changed my mind. I umm, I just want you to help me forget about the troubles of this world. I want you to help me forget about what's bothering me. That's all I want."

"And then what? When we're done, you're just going to wallow out of here and cry about the truth."

"Yes, until we can meet again."

"This isn't right, Sonja."

"I know, but it feels perfect, doesn't it."

I shook my head. Not because she was wrong about her statement, but because I was wrong for falling into her trap, I was a grown ass man, yet she used her charm on me like I was just a little boy. An infant that smiled at everything she said.

"Sonja, I like you. I don't want to hurt you anymore then I've already done."

"Hurt me." She laughed. "You didn't hurt me, you freed me, Xzavier. I was being held captive by a woman who wanted something that she didn't need. I was hiding inside of myself until I met you. Locking myself into a marriage that was extorting me of the real me. You freed me, Xzavier.

When I'm with you, I'm free. When I'm with Donnie, I used to feel captivated. Now, I feel like I'm being held captive."

"So, that's his name, Donnie. Donnie's your husband?" I asked.

"Yes, he is."

"How long have you two been married?"

"Long enough to know we should have just stayed friends."

"Yet, you love him."

"Yes, I do. But love isn't all a marriage needs. Love is just the first step. In order to climb the ladder, you need support, honesty, romance, time, effort, and patience. And I've supported him in all that he's done, but he hasn't been honest with me. The effort he's put into our marriage has made my patience run thin."

I shook my head. I wasn't married, and I've never been married so I didn't know what to say, or what to feel. But I did know what love was, and she was right! Love was only the beginning. The foundation. You had to have a lot more to begin to build.

"So, even after all of that you said, what made you come here? Why tell me you're married now?"

"I don't know. It's just. I don't want to hurt you, Xzavier. You deserve the best in life, and the hand I've been dealt, it's forcing me to call you all in or…"

"Or, what?" I asked, unsure of where she was going with this.

"Or you have to fold," she said as she finally looked into my eyes. I saw something in her eyes as she talked. It wasn't pain, it was betrayal. Pain was just the mask for betrayal. She was betraying someone or something. Her marriage, her husband. She had laid down with a man she wanted to be with, yet she had to sleep in the bed with a man she wish she never knew.

"Fold, what exactly?" I asked. Sonja snatched her hand away from mine and stood to her feet.

"Do you remember the passage in the Bible where God was telling them that he had so much more that he wanted to tell them, but he knew they weren't ready to hear it, to actually know it."

I nodded as I looked at her.

"I have so much that I want to tell you, that I need to tell you, but I'm not sure if you can handle it."

I stood to my feet and walked up to her. She took a step backwards, not just yet ready to be in my embrace. Still rebuilding the walls that I had knocked down. Cementing them, making them stronger to where this time I'd have to work overtime just to break them down.

"I can handle everything that comes my way, as long as were hand in hand to fight it off together."

Sonja faced me as she looked into my eyes. "Can you make my pain go away? Can you free me like you did only hours ago? Take me to your fantasy even though we're not on your island, and no matter what I promise to keep it Behind Closed Doors."

I walked up to her and wiped her tears from her cheek. Our lips found each other's as our tongues removed any words from being exchanged. She was a great kisser, a challenging one, and I was always up for a challenge. I removed her housecoat and rubbed her shoulders. I did my best to ease her pain. She melted as we kissed for what felt like hours. Sonja removed my shirt over my head as she rubbed her nails along my chest. She didn't need an invitation, not a room full of spectators, only me. I removed her silk pajama bottoms as she stood in front of me with a set of purple Victoria Secret panties on that revealed her most deepest secrets.

I pulled her to me, hugging her as we danced to the beat of our own drum. The woman that I held in my arms was a woman that I was head over heels for, yet she was married. Donnie was her husband, and I was her escape. A love triangle that was formed into a perfect shape.

"Sonja," I called her name.

"Yes," she answered.

"Do you think it's possible to love two different people at the same time?" I asked

"Yes," she said.

"How?"

"You love them for two different reasons."

"What reason do you love him?"

"I love him because I promised to even when times get hard."

"Do you love me?" I wanted to know.

"I do."

"Why?"

"I love you because you allowed me to. Because before I knew your name you saw through me. You let me be you, and you let me help you be you. Every time I'm with you, I feel safe, wanted, desired and appreciated."

"You don't feel that with your husband?"

"No. When I'm with Donnie, I feel trapped, and sometimes I feel alone. Even when he's in the same room with me."

"Yet you stayed with him, why?"

"Because, I felt that with him is where I belonged.

"Yet, you're here, with me."

"Because, this is where I want to be, with you."

I looked into Sonja's eyes. I was looking for something, searching for something. I was hoping I could find it, so I looked deeper. All I was looking for was a glimmer of hope, the truth. I knew she was holding back. She had already told me. And she was right, it might've been something that I couldn't handle. I just hope whatever it was, whenever she found the courage to tell me, that I would be able to accept it.

"Take you panties off," I demanded.

I caught her by surprise with my demand, but she did as I told her. Sonja stepped out of her panties and pulled her shirt over her head. She unhooked her bra and let it fall freely to the ground. She stood before me naked. She was beautiful. She was right. I did want her, I desired her, and God knew I appreciated every inch of her being. The good and the bad. The truth, and the secrets.

"Bend over the arm of the couch," I demanded as I eased my briefs down my legs. I let them fall to the floor then I stepped out of them. Sonja took orders well as she sashayed over to the couch and placed her hands on the arm as she bent over spacing her feet. Her apple bottom was perfect.

I see why God used an apple for the truth in the bible. Her apple bottom was supposed to be forbidden fruit to me. She was married, bound to a man by only two words, I do.

I walked behind her as I stroked my dick to its strongest potential. She wanted me to ease her pain, so I was going to do just that.

"Don't scream, just take this dick, okay, "I said as I lined myself up with her hole.

Sonja nodded as she gripped the edge of the couch for support. I used my dick to rub along her slit, juicing her with her own cream. After I got her nice and wet, I slammed home in one thrust. Sonja's head flung back as a yelp escaped her mouth.

"Umm, fuck!" She screamed as I fucked her hard and fast deep strokes with each thrust. I hit her walls as I bounced around inside of her. I hated when I had to work hard to take a woman's walls down. I was upset. She had lied to me with nothing but the truth. She was married to another man, Donnie. I wondered what he was like. Did he fuck her rough like I was doing right now? Did he make her scream like she was doing now? Did he make her pussy wet like it was now?

I gripped her as cheeks and spread them giving me more room to go deeper. And deeper I went as I continued to fuck her hard, forcing her over the arm of the couch as she screamed and moaned at the same time. She wanted me, yet she wanted him too. She wanted peace, yet the pain I was feeding her felt good. She was lost, confused in my dick game. All I wanted to do was clear her mind, free her from her torment of loving two men at one time, so that she could make her decision a little easier.

I slammed home at a fast, hard pace. It seemed as if the more pain I took away from her, the more pain I felt on the inside. I pounded her pussy to ease my own pain. Her pussy creamed all over my dick as I rammed her hard. She was halfway over the arm of the couch as I pinned her to it.

"Oh God, Xzavier, shit babe!" she screamed as I plunged in and out of her.

"Say it, Sonja!" I said as I slapped her ass hard enough to leave a mark.

"Oooo, fuck! Say what?" she asked as my dick left her confused.

"Tell me the truth," I said as I slapped her ass again."

"I can't," she moaned.

Her answer only made me madder. I rammed her pussy deep with one hard thrust and held my dick at the bottom of her pussy. Then, I repeated the process as she screamed out she was sorry. Her pussy was dripping wet, wanting me to keep going. It was wanting me to punish it for its betrayal. Sonja's head fell forward as she moaned and begged for me to keep going.

I continued to ram her hard and said, "I can do this all night long, I promise. Tell me!" I spat.

"I love you, Xzavier!" she cried out as she fell over the arm of the couch. That wasn't the answer I was looking for, but it was all I needed to hear at that moment as I came inside of her.

Chapter 21
The Next Day
Xzavier

I woke up with a strange smile on my face. I was fully complete from the sex session Sonja and I had last night, yet I felt that I had left some questions unanswered. There was a bunch of questions that I got incorrect, yet I still felt that I passed her test. She left my home fully satisfied when I walked her to the door, but as soon as she opened her car door, she pulled her walls back up, hiding whatever she had to tell me so she could go back to her happy husband so that she could stay sad and undesired. I didn't understand marriage, and I damn sure didn't understand women.

I eased out of bed and to get ready for the day. My father was holding a meeting for the mother board and the Deacon board members to discuss our annual picnic. I was looking forward to the picnic, only because Sonja and her praise dance team was supposed to be performing. Sonja. God how she impacted my life in such a passionate way. We were both living a double life. The life we let the world see seemed perfect, seemed worth living. But the life we hid from the world, the life we enjoyed the most, it was the life we really wanted. A life of romance, a life of passion and sex. A life with each other.

As I got out the shower, I checked my phone for any message from Sonja, even a missed call. But there was nothing from her. I tossed my phone back on the stand and finished getting dressed for the meeting.

As I was getting dressed, my phone chimed with a text message notification. I grabbed my phone and looked at the screen. There was a text from an unknown number. I opened the message. I looked at the screen, the message said to check my mailbox. I finished getting dressed, then I walked outside to my mailbox. I opened the black mailbox to see a manilla envelope inside. I grabbed the envelope. The envelope was addressed to me, with no return name or address. I opened the envelope and pulled out the thin contents inside. I flipped the pages over. I looked at the images. The images were of me and Sonja.

We weren't smiling, in fact, Sonja was crying. We were dressed for the occasion on the pictures. We were both naked, dressed in each other sweat and juices. We were joined together like we were married. It was lustful matrimony. I looked at the images. There were multiple images of us, each one a different facial expression. Even though we had on masquerade masks, I knew who were on the images. I could never forget the face she made when I was inside of her. I looked at the last image. This one was different from the rest. This image had writing in red ink. It said to have twenty thousand dollars sent to a specific P.O. box by Saturday night, or the images would be put out for the world to see. I did the calculation in my head. Whoever it was wanted the money the night of our annual fundraiser picnic. I didn't have twenty grand to just hand over. Hell, I didn't have twenty grand at all. I looked at the images again. Sonja was so beautiful in each one. A beautiful nightmare.

I walked inside my father's church to find that everyone was there waiting on me. I had sat in my car sending countless text messages to Sonja explaining to her what I found in my mailbox. Sonja didn't reply to any of my messages, but thanks to Apple iPhone, I was able to see that she read each and every message. I hated being left on read.

"Xzavier, good to see you show up. We've been waiting on you," My father said.

I nodded as I took my seat beside him. "Sorry I'm late everyone. I got stuck in traffic," I said bringing laughter to the room.

"Okay, ladies and gentlemen. This weekend is our twentieth annual Save A Soul fundraiser. Every year we have brought in enough money to put towards our Save A Soul orphanage home. Our goal this year will be at least twenty thousand dollars. The money will go towards getting more beds for the orphanage home, and school clothes and school materials for the kids. Do anyone have any ideas for this year?"

"We can have a face painting booth," Sister Johnson said. Everyone nodded as my father jotted her idea down.

"That's good, Sister Johnson. Anyone else?"

"A kissing booth, on the cheek that is," Monica said, smiling.

"A kissing booth?" My father said as he laughed. "I guess a kiss on the cheek is manageable."

"I can make some pies and cakes to sell," Sister Dortha insisted.

"You know how everyone loves you pies, Sister Dortha. You know I'll buy an entire pie by myself," my father said as he jotted down her idea.

"What about a sack race?" I said.

A few people nodded in agreement.

"That's a good idea son. I like that." My father agreed as he wrote my idea down.

"Are the praise dance team still going to perform?" Sister Johnson asked.

I was thinking the same thing since Sonja didn't show up. Before my father got a chance to answer Sister Johnson's question, the door opened and in walks Sonja. The room fell silent at her beauty. Sonja wore her hair pulled back in a tight ponytail. Her skirt was tight, but professional. I know a few people were wondering what she looked like outside of her clothes, yet I was the only one in the room that had the honor of knowing firsthand.

Rudy nudged me in my side.

I leaned over as he whispered, "She's something special, huh?"

I found myself getting a little jealous as Rudy stared at Sonja. I knew the thoughts he was planting in his mind. It was the same thoughts I had planted in my mind when I first laid eyes on her.

"Ms. Echols, glad that you could make it. We were just talking about your performance. That's if you're still up to it?" My father asked.

Sonja took her seat, far away from me. She didn't even acknowledge me.

"Yes, we are all prepared for the picnic. I'm looking forward to our first performance."

My father smiled. "Okay, that sums up our annual picnic. I want to thank everyone for coming. We have cake and refreshments in the cafeteria if anyone is hungry," my father said as he stood up. Everyone began to shake hands and some hugged as we all departed the room.

The entire time my eyes were on Sonja as she talked with Sister Johnson.

I waited a short distance away for her to finish her conversation. As she finished talking, Rudy beat me to the punch as he walked up to Sonja. I could hear him introducing himself. He shook her hand and brought it to his lips to kiss it. It was then that Sonja eyes caught mines. She pulled her hand back as if she had been caught cheating. She held my stare for a brief moment, then she excused herself to leave the room. As she walked past me, I turned to see her leave.

Rudy stood beside me and said, "Ummm, the Devil does wear Prada," he said then laughed.

Sonja

I knew me walking past Xzavier would stir something deep in his soul. I wasn't ignoring him to be an asshole, I just didn't have anything to say at the moment. Last night, when I got home Donnie was waiting on me in our bedroom. He had the TV on, and when I first walked in the room, I thought he was watching a porn movie but when I looked at the screen, it was the video of me and Xzavier at Xzavier's club. What started out as a mission to clear Donnie's debt ended up being one big game to him. Donnie made it very clear, if I didn't get the money, he needed to pay his debts off, he would send the video to Pastor King, and ruin their family image. Donnie knew that I had somewhere in the process of letting Xzavier inside of me, he really found his way inside of my heart. The only place I was supposed to keep him out of.

As I snapped back to reality, Xzavier came up behind me. I knew it was him. I was familiar with his sweet Gucci cologne. He stood directly beside me, never looking at me, but seeing right through me.

"I was sure we were too old for games, Sonja."

"Who says I'm playing any kind of game with you?" I said, never looking at him.

"Well, whatever it is you're doing, it isn't working," he said, barely raising his voice.

I turned to look at him. "Xzavier, you know I'm married. We can't do this in the open like this."

He sighed. "You wasn't married last night, were you?" he spat.

I huffed as his low blow caught me in the stomach. "Okay, you know what," I said as began to walk off.

Xzavier softly gripped my arm, stopping me in my tracks. "I'm sorry," he said as he looked into my eyes. "This whole thing, us. It's different. I've never caught feelings for any woman long enough to realize it. And you being married makes it that much harder. I want to make it work, but you being married limits my ability to do so. Then the way you look at me, it's taunting me to dare. It's making me want to go harder for you."

"Don't, Xzavier. You'll only complicate things."

"Too late. Since the first moment I laid eyes on you, my life hasn't been any easier. But I can deal with it, I promise. The hard part is knowing that you want what I want, but you're too afraid to fight for it."

I shook my head. "Xzavier, please," I said as he touched the bottom of my chin bringing my eyes up to his.
"You don't have to explain anything to me. I know how you feel towards me. But you should explain to your husband how you feel about him. Look, I'm hosting another party tomorrow night. You don't need an invitation; I hope to see you there."

Xzavier kissed me softly on the cheek and walked away without looking back.

I took a deep breath as I watched him go towards his office. It took everything in me not to go after him. For him to lay me across his desk and make sweet devilish love to me. I held my ground in the end. I couldn't let him have me anymore then he already has. His love making wasn't making it any easier, and Donnie wasn't either. Donnie had given me a plan, but I had revised it.

Xtasy

When the picnic was over, so would we be.

Chapter 22
Xzavier

I sent out numerous invitations for tonight, but there was only one person I was really hoping would show. The place was packed, and to my amazement, no one needed any help getting the party started tonight. Normally, I would be in the mood to help someone bring out their fantasy, but tonight I wasn't in the mood. As I went to my office, I received another text from the random number. This time it wasn't just pictures, it was an entire video of Sonja and I's session. The words under the video said to make sure I came through on my end of the deal. A deal that I didn't agree to. But I had no choice, did I? My father's legacy was in the middle of my sticky situation. I had gotten everything I wanted, yet I had given up so much in return. If my father was to find out what I was doing behind closed doors, he would have a heart attack. He would probably even disown me. My father has been supportive of everything I've ever done, but if he was to find out about the club, I would lose him altogether.

The stress put me in a deep sleep. I woke up by the sound of my alarm. I sat up in my office chair and looked around. The club was almost empty. I walked to my office door and looked out the glass. All that was left was a few bartenders, and the cleanup crew. I suppose the night was another success, for everyone else that is. I huffed as I turned to go back to my desk. I turned on my speaker and let the tracks play at will. As the beat began to play, The Isley Brothers slowly sang my pain away.

'Can I go on my way without you/ ohhhh how can I know/ If I go on my way without you/ ohhhh where would I go/ Set sail with me/ mystic lady, set my spirit free/ new love to find and though I leave a lover behind/ I'll always come back to you'.

The Isley Brothers Voyage to Atlantis played as I let my head fall to my chest.

"Did I miss the party?" Sonja's voice sweetly sounded behind me.

I turned to the woman that made me lukewarm. One minute she had me hot, and the next she made me want to put my heart on ice. She was beautiful, even with her masquerade mask on. She stepped inside my office and closed the door behind me. I stood behind my desk, nervously trying to gather my thoughts.

"You came," I said, nervously.

"Sorry I'm late. I had to sneak out." She laughed. Sonja began to nod her head to the music. "I haven't heard this song in years," she said as she snapped her fingers.

I sat in my chair as I watched her sing to the music.

"She's my lady, now and ever. Ohh how can I know. Can we go all the way together, ohhh ~~" Sonja sung to me as she walked up to me. The way she sung made me think that she was the creator of the song.

"I was at home in the bed with the man that I 'd married, and while he was asleep, I looked at him."

"And what did you see?" I asked as I opened up my legs for her to step between them.

"I didn't see the man I fell in love with years ago," she said as she looked down at me with love in her eyes.

"And you seeing that made you come here?"

"No, he had nothing to do with why I'm here tonight."

"Then, what brought you here?" I asked as she slow danced between my legs.

"Xzavier, you know I do more than just dance, right?" she said changing the subject.

"Uhm, I didn't know that, but what does that have to do with anything?" I asked curiously.

Sonja walked over to my stereo and turned it down. She had her back to me as she began to sing softly. I couldn't make out the words as she sung under her breath, until her voice began to boom like she was performing at a sold-out concert.

"I bow down to pray I try to make the worse seem better/ Lord show me the way/ to cut through all this worn-out leather/ I got a

hundred million reasons to walk away/ but baby I just need one good one to stay!" Sonja sung as she stared into my eyes.

Her message was clear as a brand-new glass window. I stood up as Sonja continued to sing her love and truth to me. She had chosen the perfect song, for a perfect moment. As she was singing, tears began to fall down her face. I knew her bearing her truth was painful, yet necessary. I pulled her into my embrace as she continued to sing.

Bow down to pray/ I try to make the worse seem better/ Loord show me the way/ to cut through all this worn-out leather/ I got a hundred million reasons to walk awayy/ but baby I just need/ onee!" her words broke up as she opened her heart to me.

I kissed her forehead as she cried on my chest. Sonja had done her part, and now it was time for me to do mines. I had to be a man and tell her husband that I was sweeping his wife off her heavy feet and taking her home with me, and this time for good.

Xtasy

Chapter 23
Donnie

Last night I slept like a king. I woke up to find Sonja's side empty, again. But it didn't bother me none. I was sure she was probably at Xzavier's house buttering him up for today. Today was Pastor King's Annual picnic fundraiser. It would be the first I will ever attend, and probably my last. Today would be the deadline that Fish gave me to have all of his money. And if everything went well with Sonja, I would have it all, maybe even a little more.

I took a quick shower to get the sleep out of my eyes. I checked my phone to see if Sonja had checked in. She hadn't. I wasn't sure what to wear so I settled for a pair of jeans and a blue V-neck to match. I didn't want to stand out, so I didn't wear any fancy jewelry. I sent a quick text to Sonja letting her know I was leaving the house, and that I would see her there, hopefully.

The drive to the church was short. Looking at Pastor King's church, by the size of it I was sure that he wouldn't miss the money once it was gone. I knew he made over twenty grand alone with just the tithe and offerings. What was one more offering for a man that was in dire need. For a picnic, the parking lot was almost packed. It took me a minute to find a parking spot. I parked beside a Toyota Camry and checked my phone for a response from Sonja.

Seeing that she hadn't replied, I stepped out the car and looked up at the sky. I knew praying to God to help me steal from a church was way out of line, but I was desperate. Desperate times called for desperate measures. I looked at people as they passed me by. Little kids were with their parents smiling, anxious to play all of the games that laid before them.

As I walked to the center of the picnic, I looked around for Sonja. With her not being home when I left, I wasn't sure what she would have on. So much was going on that it was hard to make out who was who.

"Hey sir, I haven't seen you here before. Are you new to the church?" A heavyset man that resembled Pastor T.D. Jakes said as he was handing me a cup of juice.

"I umm, yes, I'm new here. I'm Donnie Echols," I said introducing myself.

"Donnie Echols, you wouldn't happen to be related to Sonja Echols, would you?" he asked.

"Yes, I am. In fact, she's my wife. I was looking for her, have you seen her?"

"If I'm not mistaken, she's in the gym getting ready to perform. I'm sorry I didn't introduce myself properly. My name is Pastor King," Pastor King said as he held his hand out.

I shook his hand and gave him a friendly smile. "It's a blessing to meet you. You have a beautiful church, pastor."

"If you think it's nice on the outside, you have to let me give you a tour on the inside," he insisted.

This was like taking candy from a baby. "After you, sir," I said as I took a sip from my cup. I smiled from behind the plastic cup as we walked past everyone inside the church.

"Is this your first picnic?" Pastor King asked.

"In fact, it is. My wife told me about it, and I had the day off, so I figured, hey why not come and show some support. You said she was going to perform?" I asked as I walked behind him.

"She's our praise dance instructor. This would be her first time performing."

"Praise dance, huh. I can tell you she's a great actor, so I'm sure you won't be disappointed."

I'm sure she'll do a fine job. Every year we put together an annual Save A Soul picnic to fund our foster home. Every year we raise over fifteen grand. This year we aim to raise at least twenty thousand, or more if God is willing."

"That's amazing, the work you're doing in the community. I'd be honored to help the cause, I too was an orphan," I said as I laid it on thick. I pulled out my wallet and handed him five hundred dollars in crips hundreds.

"This is a generous donation, Mr. Echols. God see's your heart, thank you," he said as he passed the money to an usher who was walking around with a bucket collecting donations.

"Thank you," I said as I watched the usher as she took the bucket to the back room.

"Pastor, I think that juice is knocking on the front door. Can you point me in the right direction of the men's room?"

Pastor King laughed and said, "Right down that hallway, second door to the left." he pointed.

I nodded as I took off in the direction of the men's room. As I made it down the hallway, I watched as an usher took the bucket of donations into a room. I walked by the room as the door was closing. I looked inside as I walked past. There were four women inside counting up all the money. I shook my head as I walked inside the men's room. This was going to be harder than I thought.

Xzavier

It felt good to wake up next to a beautiful woman. Not just any beautiful woman either. Sonja, the most beautiful woman I've ever laid eyes on. Last night as she opened her heart to me, I eased my way inside of it. The place where I belonged. We made love all night long, and when we got done, we put out heads together to figure out how we were going to break the news to her so-called husband. Sonja kept telling me that she wanted to tell me something, but she never said exactly what it was. It seemed that we both were hiding something that we wanted to tell each other. It was only a matter of time before the truth was exposed. Like my mother always told me, what's done in the dark comes to light.

I arrived at the annual picnic in high fashion. It was days like this that I reflected my father. I have to say I got my swag from my father. I stepped out my car in a Tom Ford V-neck, with a pair of all-white Tom Ford shorts; a pair of white Tom Ford loafers with the tan bubble gum bottom. I walked up to the picnic with all eyes on me like Tupac. My mother was the first to greet me.

"Hey son, don't you look ravishing today? Either you're looking for a wife, or a modeling gig." She laughed.

I hugged her and kissed her cheek. "I won't say that I'm looking for a wife, because I think she found me."

My mother placed her hand over her mouth in surprise. She pushed me playfully and said, "She found you. Who is this she that you haven't brought home for your mother to meet?"

I smiled like I was a little kid. "I know ma, and I'm sorry. She's here, I think. You'll meet her today, I promise," I said as I kissed her cheek again.

I looked around as a few of the women in the choir looked at me in awe.

"Where's dad?" I asked looking around for him.

"The last time I saw him, he was showing the place to some man. You know you father. He's always trying to get new members to join the church."

I nodded as I looked around for Sonja. I texted her phone to let her know that I was here, and that I was looking for her. I waited for a brief second to see if she would read the message. When she didn't, I placed my phone back in my pocket.

"I'm going to go and look for dad to let him know I made it."

"Okay honey. Tell your father to meet me at the dunk tank. He knows it's his year to get inside the tank. Deacon Sprite will end up falling asleep up there, and we can't have him drowning around all these kids."

I laughed at her comment. "Okay, I will ma," I said as she walked off in the direction of a group of little girls. I went in the opposite direction to find my father; and Sonja.

Chapter 24
Sonja

Last night with Xzavier was amazing. One of the best nights of my entire life to be exact. Xzavier let me open up to him, and when I did, he wrapped his arms around me and molded me into his heart. He was everything a woman could want in a man. Everything that I deserved. He was the better life that I had prayed for. The greener grass that people talk about on the other side.

Last night, I realized that it was time to end things with Donnie. I didn't tell Xzavier about what Donnie had planned, or about what Donnie had asked of me. I had made up my mind. I wasn't going to go through with Donnie's plan. In fact, I had a plan of my own.

After I left Xzavier's house this morning, I devised a plan to save myself from an eternal lake of fire. I made a deal with God, forget what me and the devil had going on before. I told God that I would do the right thing as long as he forgave me for breaking my vows.

I arrived at Pastor Kings picnic. There was music playing for the kids, Christian rap music. I was due to do perform my first praise dance rehearsal with the kids. I was anxious to do it, but there was something else on my mind. My phone chimed in my purse. I pulled it out and look at the message from Xzavier. He always made me smile when I was feeling down. There was another message from Donnie as well. He infuriated my soul in the worse way. I tossed my phone back in my purse as I walked up to the picnic. I noticed Sister King as she was talking to a group of young women. Most of them were due to perform with me later today. I walked up to say hello.

"Hey, Sister King, you all did an amazing job with everything."

Sister King hugged me as she always did. "Thank You, Ms. Echols. I'm glad that you could make it. And I must say that we are all looking forward to your first performance, right ladies?"

My dance team all nodded with smiles on their faces.

"They all worked so hard on the routine. I know you'll be proud of them all," I said as I hugged each and every one of them.

I looked around for Xzavier, but he was nowhere in sight.

175

"Looking for someone?" Sister King asked.

"Uhm, I, no ma'am." I lied. "I was just taking in all the events."

"Oh, we may need your help with something else also," she said.

"Anything, you just name it."

"Sister Maxey didn't make it. She caught a summer cold so she won't be able to do the kissing booth. Do you think you can fill in for her, until your performance?"

"Of course. I'll go to the ladies' room and I'll head right over."

"Okay, there is already a long line waiting, so hurry back."

I nodded as I walked off in the direction of the main church. I wanted to see Xzavier, but if he was to see me before I finished the job, he could ruin everything. I eased inside, stopping abruptly as I noticed Pastor King talking with his back to me. My aim was to make it to the ladies room, which was in the same hallway as the accountant room. The same room where Xzavier made Sister Johnson pay her tithes.

Pastor King laughed as I was doing my best to sneak past him unnoticed. All of a sudden his laughter stopped, and so did I. I had a feeling that he was looking directly- at me, like a motion sensor camera. And he was.

"Ms. Echols," Pastor King spoke.

I closed my eyes and took a deep breath. I felt like I was sneaking in the house on a school night after my curfew.

"Oh heyyy, Pastor King. I didn't see you there," I said as I turned to give him a hug.

"Were you looking for your husband?" he asked, taking me by surprise.

"My-my husband?" I stuttered.

"Yes, I met him a little earlier. He seems like a good man. You have to bring him by the church for service this Sunday. It's going to be a good one." He smiled as he clasped his hands together.

"I will, Pastor. Did you see which way my husband went?" I asked as I looked around for him.

"I think he said he was going to the men's room. I think that punch is getting the best of everyone." he laughed.

I laughed as I looked towards the restrooms. If I knew Donnie any better, he was on the same mission as me, but for two different reasons. "Let me go check and make sure he's okay. I'll see you later, Pastor," I said, excusing myself.

I looked down the hallway in the direction of the restrooms. It seemed farther away than it ever was. I took a deep breath as I eased down the hallway. I prayed that I didn't bump into Donnie.

I walked in the ladies room and walked up to the sink. I turned on the water as I cuffed my hand under the faucet. I cleaned my hands as if I was washing the blood of Jesus off of them. I couldn't believe I was about to sin in the house of the Lord. I sighed as I turned the water off. I grabbed a few paper towels from the holder and dried my hands.

As I was placing the paper towels in the trash, an older woman looked at me from the mirror and said, "Baby, whatever's bothering you, just know God is never late. He's always on time."

I smiled a fake smile as I nodded my head. This would be the only time that I prayed that God would be late. I walked out the restroom with my head down. My shoulders were too heavy to carry both. As I lifted my head, the men's restroom door opened.

"Babe," Donnie smiled.

Xzavier

I was stopped more times than I could count as I maneuvered through the crowds to find my father. I finally found him walking down the hallway leading to his office. And not only did I find him, but I found Sonja, too.

"Father, another success," I said as I shook his hand. I looked at Sonja as she stood beside a man around my height, but taller, and stockier. He wore this grim smile on his face. Like he knew something that I didn't know and he wasn't going to tell me even if I asked, even if I begged.

"Indeed son, another success. I know you know Ms. Echols. Come to find out, she's a Mrs. And this is her husband, Mr. Echols," My father introduced.

"You can call me, Donnie," Sonja's husband said as he stuck his hand out for me to shake.

I gave him a half smile as I shook his hand with a firm grip. I wanted him to feel the same firm grip that I used to hold his wife tight and close to me last night as she slept in my bed wishing I was him.

"Xzavier," I replied.

We held our grip for a second, looking into each other's eyes the whole time.

"I've heard a lot about you. My wife speaks very highly of you. I heard you're an entrepreneur."

I let his hand go as I looked at his wife. Sonja's head fell to her chest as she took a deep breath.

"Oh God, I should be at the kissing booth. I don't want to let all those people waiting in line down," Sonja said smiling. She grabbed Donnie's hand and said, "Come on babe, I may need your protection from the younger guys." She laughed, as well as my father.

I didn't find any of it funny. Her words brought pain and torment to my life.

Just hearing her call him babe. That was worse than a knife going through my back.

Donnie smiled at me as Sonja pulled him in her direction. "It was very nice to meet you, Xzavier. I'll be seeing you around, right?"

There was so much emphasis on the word, 'right'. I knew right then and there who had sent the pictures to my house. I looked at Sonja, the woman that I had fell head over heels for. She was looking back at me with sympathy in her eyes. She looked as if she was feeling sorry for me. But I wasn't the one who was pulling someone in my direction who I was dying to push away.

"I guess you will," I said as I looked at Sonja.

"Donnie, come on," Sonja pleaded.

Donnie smiled as he saluted my father on the way by.

178

I sighed as they were both out of sight.

"Son, what was that all about?" My father asked as he walked to his office. I walked inside and closed the door behind myself.

"What was what about?" I said as I sat down across from him.

"Son, do you know what a parable is?" My father asked.

"Of course, pops. You taught me how to read through them, and not just read them," I said.

"Exactly! So, if I taught you how to interpret parables, what makes you think I don't know what a parable is?" my father spat.

"What are you getting at, father?" I asked.

"I'm getting at the truth if you'll stop hiding behind the lie."

I sighed. "What do you want me to say, pops?"

"You don't have to say anything. But what I would like for you to say is that you haven't slept with that man's wife. Now that would be pleasing to my ears."

"Then, don' t make me lie to you, pops."

My father sat down as he wiped the sweat from his brow. "Son, why? There's so many other beautiful single women out there that you could've went after."

"But there's none like her, pops! Trust me, she's one of a kind," I said raising my voice.

"That may be the case, but she's not yours, and as long as she's bounded by oath by God, she will never be."

I shook my head as his words sunk in deeper than a virus with no cure. Without her, I felt as if I would die. With her, I felt alive. I hated her oath. I hated that she went to the altar with him. I wished that she had left him at the altar alone, stranded with no way of contact ever again. But she didn't. She had said I do when she knew damn well she didn't. At least, now she doesn't.

"What do I do, pops? I need your help, please," I begged.

"You do the right thing," he said.

"And what's that?"

"You let her decide what she really wants. If she really loves him, she'll act like she never met you. She'll act like whatever you two did in the past never happened. But, if somehow she wants you, and she don't want her husband, then she has to come clean. She has to be a woman, and tell him that she wants a divorce."

What my father said was the honest to God truth. But I don't think God really knew what he did when he ordained marriage as the sacred commitment. To me you don't need a ring and a preacher to say you love someone and that you want to spend the rest of your life with them. I knew I loved Sonja the very first moment I laid eyes on her. I didn't have a ring, just her beautiful face, and my shocked face. She was the most beautiful chocolate bar a man could ever crave. But she was like forbidden sweets, and I was the man with sugar diabetes. Too much of her could kill me. And I was dying slowly.

Chapter 25
Sonja

"Donnie, could you behave yourself today, please!" I said as we made it outside by the kissing booth.

Donnie smiled with his hands in his pockets. I thought I had married the man of my dreams, but in reality, I married the man of a living nightmare. "What, I am behaving myself." he smiled.

I huffed and shook my head. I was so over him, and so over his whole plot. I stepped in the kissing booth and opened the curtain to see a long line of young boys and teenagers with their tickets in hand, ready to give me a big juicy kiss on the cheek.

I sat in the chair and scooted it to the front of the booth. I placed a big bogus smile on my face and said, "Hello my little knight in shining armor, would you please come and save me from this here booth by placing a kiss on my cheek?"

The little boy, who couldn't have been no more than ten years old smiled from ear to ear innocently as he stood on his tippy toes and handed me his ticket which costed him only fifty cents. I thought about what this kiss would cost the little boy. Then, I thought about what me kissing Xzavier would cost us both. The little boy was innocent. But me and Xzavier were two grown adults that knew right from wrong. We were guilty as charged.

"You ready little man?" I asked as I leaned over the booth. He smiled and nodded. I wondered if he would remember this day, his first kiss, if I was his first. The little boy leaned forward and kissed me softly on the cheek. His lips were so small I could barely feel them.

When I looked at him, he stood staring at me shy like. He ran away as if he were about to go and tell all of his friends. There was another little boy in line waiting for his kiss. He looked to be about the same age as the one before.

"Ma'am, can you close your eyes, so that it'll feel real?" he asked smiling innocently. I smiled back at him and closed my eyes.

I turned my cheek just a tad so that he could get a good kiss on the cheek. I waited for a second just to feel his small lips. His lips touched mines, and it caught me by surprise. His lips weren't small like the little boy before, his lips were full, like a grown man. People around us gasped, which caused me to open my eyes. The little boy was standing behind a man that I had grown to love

Xzavier's lips felt perfect as he kissed me like no one was around us. I broke our kiss away and looked around for Donnie, who was nowhere in sight.

"Xzavier, what are you doing?" I asked as I locked eyes with his mother.

"I'm claiming what's mine. Where's your ex-husband?" Xzavier asked.

He brought a smile to my face by calling Donnie my ex-husband. I shrugged and said, "I don't know, he was just here a few minutes ago."

Xzavier's mother walked up beside us. "You two have a lot of explaining to do," she said with her arms crossed. Pastor King stood right beside her.

"Mom, I can explain," I said as I grabbed Sonja's hand in mines.

"I sure hope so, because your father says that she's married, and that her husband is around here somewhere."

I looked at my father like he had betrayed me. But then again, I knew him and my mother didn't believe in secrets.

"Mrs. King, don't blame him for what's become of us, blame me. It's all my fault," I said with my head down.

"Darling, pick your head up. There's no reason to be ashamed of who you love," Mrs. King said.

"It's just that, I'm married and I know this isn't right, but it feels like it's meant to be."

"And if it is, then it'll be," Mrs. King said. "Honey, I was once just like you. I too was married, but in love with another man."

Xzavier looked at his mother in shock. "Ma', you never told me that."

"That's because I've grown out of that old love and I fell head-first into something real. Your father, before he became a preacher, he pursued me when I was married to my first love, Michael.

"Pops, is that true?" Xzavier asked.

Pastor King nodded. "It's true. I was young, and naive. I wanted what I wanted, and that's all I wanted. Your mother was a diamond, in the hands of the wrong man. We snuck around and did what God would call defying him. But your mother and I did it all wrong in the beginning, until my father, your grandfather, told me to go to her husband like a man tell him what we had been doing."

"And what happened when you did?" Xzavier asked.

"We fought in the middle of the dirt road in front of everyone we both knew. But that didn't solve anything. Your mother left us both, and we sat there on the ground looking dumb and alone, with each other."

"So, how did you two go about getting married if she left the both of you?" I asked.

"Michael and I sat in the dirt, and he told me, that he only wanted her happy, no matter who it was that caused her happiness. He said that it was up to her to decide who she gave her heart to, even if it wasn't him. So, we did just that. We went to her father's house where she was at crying, and we told her what we came up with."

"So, she just up and picked you, and Michael left?" Xzavier asked.

Pastor King laughed and shook his head. "Not exactly. She looked at us like two dumb fools, and she said to get out of her father's house. She was no woman who would be given an ultimatum of who she could and could not love."

"So, how did she end up with you?" I asked.

"It was a year later, after I had been away from home staying with my aunt in Mississippi. Your father knocked on my door and let a dozen lilies on the doorstep. I opened the door, and no one was there. He did that for a week straight, no letter, no card, no identification of who was sending them."

"How'd you know who was sending them?" I asked, smiling. I was so in love with being in love.

"I knew. Michael was never a romantic man. He never gave me flowers, or anything like that. The next time your father tried to sneak and place flowers on my doorstep, I was there waiting for him, hiding beside the house. When he tried to walk away, I called out his name. He slowly turned, seeing that he was busted. That day, I knew he was the one for me," Mrs. King said as a tear fell from her eyes.

"How did you know?" I asked.

"Because true love never gives up. It always fight, and no matter what gets in the way, it will wait until it moves," she said as Pastor King hugged and kissed her.

"So, you think I should just walk up to him and tell him how I feel about his wife?" Xzavier asked.

"Yes. Times have changed. He won't just let her go, but as long as he knows, he will know that along the line of being a husband, he failed. If he loves her, he'll fight for her, but if he doesn't, he'll ask for a divorce," Mrs. King said.

Xzavier nodded and said, "But where is he?"

I looked around and noticed that almost everyone was standing around us, and no one was paying attention to the accountant room.

Chapter 26
Donnie

I watched Sonja as she let the little boy kiss her on the cheek. The line in front of her was long. Long enough to keep her busy while I snuck away and did the job she was avoiding. I nodded as I walked past a group of older women as I made my way inside the church. It seemed as if everyone was outside taking pictures of the little boys getting their first kiss from Sonja. Perfect timing.

I walked down the hallway and stood in front of the accountant room where all the money was at. I knocked twice lightly. No one answered. I twisted the knob, just to find out the door was locked. I looked around to make sure no one was coming. Seeing that the coast was clear I pressed my shoulder to the side of the door and pushed hard. The door moved, but barely. I applied a little more pressure and shoved my shoulder into the side of the door. The door swung open as the trimming from the side of the door flew off.

I stepped in the hallway making sure no one heard my intrusion. Seeing that I was alone, I ran inside and looked around for the money that I came for. There were buckets of money on the desk, dollar bills and change from a variety of dead presidents. I rubbed my hands together to dry the sweat that had formed. There was way more money than I needed. I could pay off my debt, and try my hand at a poker tournament in Vegas, if I played my cards right.

I knew I only came for enough money to pay my debt, but the devil had taken over me. Greed, it was deeper than people understood. Then again, I was taking every dollar just to get back at Sonja. She was my wife, past tense. I'd be damned if I gave her a divorce, just so she could go and marry Xzavier. No deal. I was taking every dollar and leaving only a tip. A tip that would lead Pastor King to Xzavier's sex paradise.

I looked around for something to hide the money in. I looked in a drawer, and I hit the jackpot. Stacks of money laid in the drawer in perfect stacks. I placed the stacks on the drawer and wiped the sweat from my brow. I prayed hell wouldn't be hotter than this. I looked around for something to place the money in. Looking through the drawers, I found a brown bag. I snatched the bag up and began to fill it up. The more money I placed in the bag, the hotter it got in the room. As I filled the bag up, I stashed the rest of the money in my pockets. I left the change and a few dollars in the buckets and walked out the room. I looked back at the work I did and shook my head. The love of money was the root of all evil.

Xzavier

I stood beside Sonja as everyone around us laughed and had a blast. We were waiting until her husband showed his face so that we could expose the truth to him. Even though I knew he was the one that mailed those pictures to my house, I still didn't think he knew how I felt about her, and how she felt about me. '

'Xzavier, can we just go? We can go anywhere you want. We don't have to tell him anything." Sonja begged.

I pulled Sonja into my embrace and said, "Come on love, you don't have to be scared. I'm right here with you. I'll take all the shame and put it on my shoulders. It's my weight to carry." I kissed her forehead.

"There he goes right there," Sonja said as her husband walked out the church.

He looked like he had been working out. He was sweating so bad.

"Just let me do the talking, okay," I said.

Sonja nodded as she walked behind me.

I walked up to Donnie with Sonja tight on my tail. "Can I have a word with you, Donnie."

"Sonja, go to the car and wait for me," Donnie said with a little aggressiveness in his voice.

Sonja stood behind me as she gripped the back of my shirt.

"Donnie, I think she should stay for this," I said as a crowd began to form around us. Christian folk or not, everyone loved a little drama in their life.

"Whatever you have to say to me, I already know. I know everything that went on, and no matter what, she's still my wife. Sonja, get yo' ass in the car, now!" he yelled.

"Now wait a minute, I understand how you feel. I do. But don't you go using that kind of language on this sacred ground," my father said.

Donnie laughed. "Sacred ground, huh. Pastor, this isn't sacred. This is the devil's playground. You may be holier than thou, but your son is nothing less than the devil himself," Donnie said.

I knew where this was going. I could see it with a blind man's eyes. It was either two things, let Sonja walk away with Donnie, and lose her forever or let Donnie expose what I was all about, and risk losing my father, forever.

"Don't you go calling my son the devil because you couldn't hold on to your wife now!" My mother defended me.

"Oh really, you think it was my fault that she slept with your son. I don't think you have any idea what's really going on, do you Mrs. King?" Donnie said with a little humor in his voice.

"Son, what is this man talking about?" my mother asked.

"Okay, Donnie! I'll go with you, just, just don't say anything, please!" Sonja begged.

"Sonja, you don't have to do this. It's okay, let him talk. It has to come out one day," I said facing her.

"Dammit, whose wife are you!" Donnie said, as he reached around me and snatched Sonja by her arm.

"Ouch! You're hurting me!" Sonja said as she tried to break away from his grasp.

"Come on Donnie, you don't have to put your hands on her like that!" I said poking my chest out to him.

"Oh, so you're not only a wife slayer, but you're also a tough guy too. You go around here preaching the word of God, and in the night hours you're bringing people together to have sex in a secret location for your own amusement. You didn't tell your mom and pops about that, huh?" Donnie spat.

I hung my head in defeat as Donnie continued to rant the truth. "You bring people together so they can have sex, unprotected sex, too. Wearing those masquerade mask couldn't hide your face though, or my wife's face, could it Sonja!"

"Son, tell me this isn't true?" My father said as he looked at me with pity in his eyes.

I had nothing to say. I figured silence was better than a lie.

"He has nothing to say to you, but a lot to say to my wife, huh! Come on Sonja, and don't make me tell you again," Donnie said as he snatched Sonja up.

"Get off of me!" Sonja snatched away as she shoved Donnie. As Donnie fell to the ground, stacks and stacks of money fell to the ground beside him. There was a brown paper sack beside him with money spilling out of it.

Everyone looked at Donnie in surprise. It had to be over thirty thousand dollars on the ground.

"Fuck!" Donnie said as he stood up.

"Pastor! Pastor!" Sister Johnson said as she ran from the church to us. She stopped in front of us as she panted, catching her breath. "The money, it's all gone, well almost all of it!" Sister Johnson said as she caught her breath.

Everyone's eyes looked to Donnie, then to the money on the floor.

"I can explain," Donnie said as my father began to walk up to him.

"Oh no, I got this one!" my mother said, causing Donnie to look in her direction.

My mother cocked her fist back and hit Donnie square in his eye, knocking him to the ground. "You messed with my son, and now you messed with my God!" she said as she rubbed her sore knuckles.

Everyone around laughed as Donnie laid out on the ground on top of the money he had tried to steal.

"I'll take care of this, Pastor," Marcus, an off duty cop, and member of the church said as he called the disturbance.

"Sonja, you're going to pay for this, I'm not going down by myself," Donnie said as he was stood to his feet and placed in cuffs.

"With your dick size, they may mistake you for a woman and place you in a women's facility." Sonja teased causing all the women around to snicker. Her comment got nothing but silence from Donnie as he was escorted off the premises.

I smiled until I landed my eyes on my father. "Pops, I can explain," I said as I walked up to him.

"There's no need, son. I already knew," my father said, taking me by surprise. "You already knew? How?" I asked.

"I received an email about an invitation to a secret location, and it demanded I wear a masquerade mask. You may have made a fake email, but you never could take your name off the building's ownership list, Xzavier King." my father laughed.

I shook my head in shame. I never knew about an ownership's list. "Why didn't you say anything before now?" I asked.

"Mistakes, son. They are meant to be made, not explained. You have to make mistakes in order to learn from them. I'm your father, not God. Who am I to judge," he said bringing a smile to my face.

"So, what are you two going to do now?" My mother said as she looked at me and Sonja.

"I have an idea or two." I smiled.

Xtasy

The Final Chapter
Two Years Later
Sonja

"Ummm, daddy. Let me brush my teeth first," I said as Xzavier kissed all over me.

"It's time to get up. I have to prepare for the service."

Xzavier jumped out of the bed naked and stretched out.

I smiled and licked my lips. "Can we be late today?" I joked.

"How can the preacher of the church be late for church? Come on babe, we can shower together and waste a little time in there." He smiled.

Xzavier walked off to the bathroom and turned the shower on. I sat up in bed and smiled as I looked to my ring finger. No longer was the ring there that Donnie wed me with. There was a new ring in place, one more perfect, and meaningful. Donnie went to prison to serve a ten year sentence for burglary of a building. The judge was also a member of Pastor King's church, so Donnie got the max sentence for his crime. On top of that, he was given another charge, theft over thirty thousand dollars. He was given another five years on top of that to run stacked. He wouldn't see parole until another three years.

In the beginning he did everything to not grant me my divorce, but a judge granted it by negligence of spousal support. As soon as the divorce was granted, Xzavier got down on one knee and placed a beautiful ring on my finger. We got married last year in his father's church in front of a large congregation.

In the beginning, there were a lot of whispers about how we met, but we didn't care. Xzavier closed down Behind Closed Doors and gave his life to God for real this time. Pastor King stepped down from the podium last year after we wed, and Xzavier took his position happily. I was now the first lady of the church, and I was happy to be. I still orchestrated the praise dance team, and we performed every first Sunday of the month.

Our marriage was beautiful, sacred. We still had fun in the bedroom, and even showed we had a very sexual marriage. But God never said a husband and wife couldn't be freaky to each other. Our favorite thing to do was make love in the dark. Because what's done in the dark always cums to light!

The End

Lock Down Publications and Ca$h Presents assisted publishing packages.

BASIC PACKAGE $499
Editing
Cover Design
Formatting

UPGRADED PACKAGE $800
Typing
Editing
Cover Design
Formatting

ADVANCE PACKAGE $1,200
Typing
Editing
Cover Design
Formatting
Copyright registration
Proofreading
Upload book to Amazon

LDP SUPREME PACKAGE $1,500
Typing
Editing
Cover Design
Formatting
Copyright registration
Proofreading
Set up Amazon account
Upload book to Amazon
Advertise on LDP Amazon and Facebook page

***Other services available upon request. Additional charges may apply
Lock Down Publications
P.O. Box 944
Stockbridge, GA 30281-9998
Phone # 470 303-9761

Submission Guideline

Submit the first three chapters of your completed manuscript to ldpsubmissions@gmail.com, subject line: Your book's title. The manuscript must be in a .doc file and sent as an attachment. Document should be in Times New Roman, double spaced and in size 12 font. Also, provide your synopsis and full contact information. If sending multiple submissions, they must each be in a separate email.

Have a story but no way to send it electronically? You can still submit to LDP/Ca$h Presents. Send in the first three chapters, written or typed, of your completed manuscript to:

LDP: Submissions Dept
Po Box 944
Stockbridge, Ga 30281

DO NOT send original manuscript. Must be a duplicate.

Provide your synopsis and a cover letter containing your full contact information.

Thanks for considering LDP and Ca$h Presents.

NEW RELEASES

IT'S JUST ME AND YOU 2 by AH'MILLION

SOUL OF A HUSTLER, HEART OF A KILLER 3 by
SAYNOMORE

THE COCAINE PRINCESS 9 by KING RIO

FOR THE LOVE OF BLOOD 3 by JAMEL MITCHELL

SANCTIFIED AND HORNY by XTASY

STRAIGHT BEAST MODE III

De'Kari

KINGPIN KILLAZ IV

STREET KINGS III

PAID IN BLOOD III

CARTEL KILLAZ IV

DOPE GODS III

Hood Rich

SINS OF A HUSTLA II

ASAD

YAYO V

Bred In The Game 2

S. Allen

THE STREETS WILL TALK II

By Yolanda Moore

SON OF A DOPE FIEND III

HEAVEN GOT A GHETTO III

SKI MASK MONEY III

By Renta

LOYALTY AIN'T PROMISED III

By Keith Williams

I'M NOTHING WITHOUT HIS LOVE II

SINS OF A THUG II

TO THE THUG I LOVED BEFORE II

IN A HUSTLER I TRUST II

By Monet Dragun

QUIET MONEY IV

EXTENDED CLIP III

THUG LIFE IV

By **Trai'Quan**

THE STREETS MADE ME IV

By **Larry D. Wright**

IF YOU CROSS ME ONCE III

ANGEL V

By **Anthony Fields**

THE STREETS WILL NEVER CLOSE IV

By K'ajji

HARD AND RUTHLESS III

KILLA KOUNTY IV

By Khufu

MONEY GAME III

By Smoove Dolla

JACK BOYS VS DOPE BOYS IV

A GANGSTA'S QUR'AN V

COKE GIRLZ II

COKE BOYS II

LIFE OF A SAVAGE V

CHI'RAQ GANGSTAS V

SOSA GANG IV

BRONX SAVAGES II

BODYMORE KINGPINS II

BLOOD OF A GOON II

By Romell Tukes

MURDA WAS THE CASE III

Elijah R. Freeman

AN UNFORESEEN LOVE IV

BABY, I'M WINTERTIME COLD III

By **Meesha**

QUEEN OF THE ZOO III

Xtasy

By **Black Migo**
CONFESSIONS OF A JACKBOY III
By Nicholas Lock
KING KILLA II
By Vincent "Vitto" Holloway
BETRAYAL OF A THUG III
By Fre$h
THE BIRTH OF A GANGSTER III
By Delmont Player
TREAL LOVE II
By Le'Monica Jackson
FOR THE LOVE OF BLOOD IV
By Jamel Mitchell
RAN OFF ON DA PLUG II
By Paper Boi Rari
HOOD CONSIGLIERE III
By Keese
PRETTY GIRLS DO NASTY THINGS II
By Nicole Goosby
LOVE IN THE TRENCHES II
By Corey Robinson
FOREVER GANGSTA III
By Adrian Dulan
THE COCAINE PRINCESS X
SUPER GREMLIN II
By King Rio
CRIME BOSS II
Playa Ray
LOYALTY IS EVERYTHING III
Molotti

Sanctified and Horny

HERE TODAY GONE TOMORROW II
By Fly Rock
REAL G'S MOVE IN SILENCE II
By Von Diesel
GRIMEY WAYS IV
By Ray Vinci
SALUTE MY SAVAGERY II
By Fumiya Payne
BLOOD AND GAMES II
By King Dream

<u>Available Now</u>

RESTRAINING ORDER **I & II**
By **CA$H & Coffee**
LOVE KNOWS NO BOUNDARIES **I II & III**
By **Coffee**
RAISED AS A GOON I, II, III & IV
BRED BY THE SLUMS I, II, III
BLAST FOR ME I & II
ROTTEN TO THE CORE I II III
A BRONX TALE I, II, III
DUFFLE BAG CARTEL I II III IV V VI
HEARTLESS GOON I II III IV V
A SAVAGE DOPEBOY I II
DRUG LORDS I II III

CUTTHROAT MAFIA I II
KING OF THE TRENCHES
By **Ghost**
LAY IT DOWN **I & II**
LAST OF A DYING BREED I II
BLOOD STAINS OF A SHOTTA I & II III
By **Jamaica**
LOYAL TO THE GAME I II III
LIFE OF SIN I, II III
By **TJ & Jelissa**
BLOODY COMMAS I & II
SKI MASK CARTEL I II & III
KING OF NEW YORK I II,III IV V
RISE TO POWER I II III
COKE KINGS I II III IV V
BORN HEARTLESS I II III IV
KING OF THE TRAP I II
By **T.J. Edwards**
IF LOVING HIM IS WRONG…I & II
LOVE ME EVEN WHEN IT HURTS I II III
By **Jelissa**
WHEN THE STREETS CLAP BACK I & II III
THE HEART OF A SAVAGE I II III IV
MONEY MAFIA I II
LOYAL TO THE SOIL I II III
By **Jibril Williams**
A DISTINGUISHED THUG STOLE MY HEART I II & III
LOVE SHOULDN'T HURT I II III IV
RENEGADE BOYS I II III IV
PAID IN KARMA I II III

Sanctified and Horny

SAVAGE STORMS I II III
AN UNFORESEEN LOVE I II III
BABY, I'M WINTERTIME COLD I II
By **Meesha**
A GANGSTER'S CODE I &, II III
A GANGSTER'S SYN I II III
THE SAVAGE LIFE I II III
CHAINED TO THE STREETS I II III
BLOOD ON THE MONEY I II III
A GANGSTA'S PAIN I II III
By J-Blunt
PUSH IT TO THE LIMIT
By **Bre' Hayes**
BLOOD OF A BOSS **I, II, III, IV, V**
SHADOWS OF THE GAME
TRAP BASTARD
By **Askari**
THE STREETS BLEED MURDER **I, II & III**
THE HEART OF A GANGSTA I II& III
By **Jerry Jackson**
CUM FOR ME I II III IV V VI VII VIII
An **LDP Erotica Collaboration**
BRIDE OF A HUSTLA **I II & II**
THE FETTI GIRLS **I, II& III**
CORRUPTED BY A GANGSTA I, II III, IV
BLINDED BY HIS LOVE
THE PRICE YOU PAY FOR LOVE I, II ,III
DOPE GIRL MAGIC I II III
By **Destiny Skai**
WHEN A GOOD GIRL GOES BAD

Xtasy

THESE NIGGAS AIN'T LOYAL **I, II & III**
By **Nikki Tee**
GANGSTA SHYT **I II &III**
By **CATO**
THE ULTIMATE BETRAYAL
By **Phoenix**
BOSS'N UP **I , II & III**
By **Royal Nicole**
I LOVE YOU TO DEATH
By **Destiny J**
I RIDE FOR MY HITTA
I STILL RIDE FOR MY HITTA
By **Misty Holt**
LOVE & CHASIN' PAPER
By **Qay Crockett**
TO DIE IN VAIN
SINS OF A HUSTLA
By **ASAD**
BROOKLYN HUSTLAZ
By **Boogsy Morina**
BROOKLYN ON LOCK I & II
By **Sonovia**
GANGSTA CITY
By **Teddy Duke**
A DRUG KING AND HIS DIAMOND I & II III
A DOPEMAN'S RICHES
HER MAN, MINE'S TOO I, II
CASH MONEY HO'S
THE WIFEY I USED TO BE I II
PRETTY GIRLS DO NASTY THINGS

Xtasy

By Nicole Goosby

TRAPHOUSE KING **I II & III**

KINGPIN KILLAZ I II III

STREET KINGS I II

PAID IN BLOOD **I II**

CARTEL KILLAZ I II III

DOPE GODS I II

By Hood Rich

LIPSTICK KILLAH **I, II, III**

CRIME OF PASSION I II & III

FRIEND OR FOE I II III

By Mimi

STEADY MOBBN' **I, II, III**

THE STREETS STAINED MY SOUL I II III

By Marcellus Allen

WHO SHOT YA **I, II, III**

SON OF A DOPE FIEND I II

HEAVEN GOT A GHETTO I II

SKI MASK MONEY I II

Renta

GORILLAZ IN THE BAY **I II III IV**

TEARS OF A GANGSTA I II

3X KRAZY I II

STRAIGHT BEAST MODE I II

DE'KARI

TRIGGADALE I II III

MURDAROBER WAS THE CASE I II

Elijah R. Freeman

GOD BLESS THE TRAPPERS I, II, III

THESE SCANDALOUS STREETS I, II, III

Sanctified and Horny

FEAR MY GANGSTA I, II, III IV, V
THESE STREETS DON'T LOVE NOBODY I, II
BURY ME A G I, II, III, IV, V
A GANGSTA'S EMPIRE I, II, III, IV
THE DOPEMAN'S BODYGAURD I II
THE REALEST KILLAZ I II III
THE LAST OF THE OGS I II III
Tranay Adams
THE STREETS ARE CALLING
Duquie Wilson
MARRIED TO A BOSS I II III
By Destiny Skai & Chris Green
KINGZ OF THE GAME I II III IV V VI VII
CRIME BOSS
Playa Ray
SLAUGHTER GANG I II III
RUTHLESS HEART I II III
By Willie Slaughter
FUK SHYT
By Blakk Diamond
DON'T F#CK WITH MY HEART I II
By Linnea
ADDICTED TO THE DRAMA I II III
IN THE ARM OF HIS BOSS II
By Jamila
YAYO I II III IV
A SHOOTER'S AMBITION I II
BRED IN THE GAME
By S. Allen
TRAP GOD I II III

RICH $AVAGE I II III

MONEY IN THE GRAVE I II III

By Martell Troublesome Bolden

FOREVER GANGSTA I II

GLOCKS ON SATIN SHEETS I II

By Adrian Dulan

TOE TAGZ I II III IV

LEVELS TO THIS SHYT I II

IT'S JUST ME AND YOU I II

By Ah'Million

KINGPIN DREAMS I II III

RAN OFF ON DA PLUG

By Paper Boi Rari

CONFESSIONS OF A GANGSTA I II III IV

CONFESSIONS OF A JACKBOY I II

By Nicholas Lock

I'M NOTHING WITHOUT HIS LOVE

SINS OF A THUG

TO THE THUG I LOVED BEFORE

A GANGSTA SAVED XMAS

IN A HUSTLER I TRUST

By Monet Dragun

CAUGHT UP IN THE LIFE I II III

THE STREETS NEVER LET GO I II III

By Robert Baptiste

NEW TO THE GAME I II III

MONEY, MURDER & MEMORIES I II III

By **Malik D. Rice**

LIFE OF A SAVAGE I II III IV

A GANGSTA'S QUR'AN I II III IV

MURDA SEASON I II III
GANGLAND CARTEL I II III
CHI'RAQ GANGSTAS I II III IV
KILLERS ON ELM STREET I II III
JACK BOYZ N DA BRONX I II III
A DOPEBOY'S DREAM I II III
JACK BOYS VS DOPE BOYS I II III
COKE GIRLZ
COKE BOYS
SOSA GANG I II III
BRONX SAVAGES
BODYMORE KINGPINS
BLOOD OF A GOON
By Romell Tukes
LOYALTY AIN'T PROMISED I II
By Keith Williams
QUIET MONEY I II III
THUG LIFE I II III
EXTENDED CLIP I II
A GANGSTA'S PARADISE
By **Trai'Quan**
THE STREETS MADE ME I II III
By **Larry D. Wright**
THE ULTIMATE SACRIFICE I, II, III, IV, V, VI
KHADIFI
IF YOU CROSS ME ONCE I II
ANGEL I II III IV
IN THE BLINK OF AN EYE
By **Anthony Fields**
THE LIFE OF A HOOD STAR

Xtasy

By Ca$h & Rashia Wilson
THE STREETS WILL NEVER CLOSE I II III
By K'ajji
CREAM I II III
THE STREETS WILL TALK
By Yolanda Moore
NIGHTMARES OF A HUSTLA I II III
BLOOD AND GAMES
By King Dream
CONCRETE KILLA I II III
VICIOUS LOYALTY I II III
By Kingpen
HARD AND RUTHLESS I II
MOB TOWN 251
THE BILLIONAIRE BENTLEYS I II III
REAL G'S MOVE IN SILENCE
By Von Diesel
GHOST MOB
Stilloan Robinson
MOB TIES I II III IV V VI
SOUL OF A HUSTLER, HEART OF A KILLER I II III
GORILLAZ IN THE TRENCHES I II III
By SayNoMore
BODYMORE MURDERLAND I II III
THE BIRTH OF A GANGSTER I II
By Delmont Player
FOR THE LOVE OF A BOSS
By C. D. Blue
MOBBED UP I II III IV
THE BRICK MAN I II III IV V

THE COCAINE PRINCESS I II III IV V VI VII VIII IX
SUPER GREMLIN
By King Rio
KILLA KOUNTY I II III IV
By Khufu
MONEY GAME I II
By Smoove Dolla
A GANGSTA'S KARMA I II III
By FLAME
KING OF THE TRENCHES I II III
by **GHOST & TRANAY ADAMS**
QUEEN OF THE ZOO I II
By **Black Migo**
GRIMEY WAYS I II III
By Ray Vinci
XMAS WITH AN ATL SHOOTER
By Ca$h & Destiny Skai
KING KILLA
By Vincent "Vitto" Holloway
BETRAYAL OF A THUG I II
By Fre$h
THE MURDER QUEENS I II III
By Michael Gallon
TREAL LOVE
By Le'Monica Jackson
FOR THE LOVE OF BLOOD I II III
By Jamel Mitchell
HOOD CONSIGLIERE I II
By Keese
PROTÉGÉ OF A LEGEND I II III

LOVE IN THE TRENCHES

By Corey Robinson

BORN IN THE GRAVE I II III

By Self Made Tay

MOAN IN MY MOUTH

SANCTIFIED AND HORNY

By XTASY

TORN BETWEEN A GANGSTER AND A GENTLEMAN

By J-BLUNT & Miss Kim

LOYALTY IS EVERYTHING I II

Molotti

HERE TODAY GONE TOMORROW

By Fly Rock

PILLOW PRINCESS

By S. Hawkins

NAÏVE TO THE STREETS

WOMEN LIE MEN LIE I II III

GIRLS FALL LIKE DOMINOS

STACK BEFORE YOU SPURLGE

FIFTY SHADES OF SNOW I II III

By A. Roy Milligan

SALUTE MY SAVAGERY

By Fumiya Payne

<u>BOOKS BY LDP'S CEO, CA$H</u>

TRUST IN NO MAN

TRUST IN NO MAN 2

TRUST IN NO MAN 3

BONDED BY BLOOD

SHORTY GOT A THUG

THUGS CRY

THUGS CRY 2

THUGS CRY 3

TRUST NO BITCH

TRUST NO BITCH 2

TRUST NO BITCH 3

TIL MY CASKET DROPS

RESTRAINING ORDER

RESTRAINING ORDER 2

IN LOVE WITH A CONVICT

LIFE OF A HOOD STAR

XMAS WITH AN ATL SHOOTER

Xtasy

9 781960 993151